Firebreak

A PARKER NOVEL

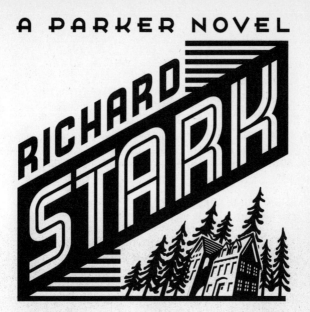

RICHARD STARK

Firebreak

Published by Warner Books

An AOL Time Warner Company

Copyright © 2001 by Richard Stark
All rights reserved.

 Mysterious Press books are published by Warner Books, Inc., 1271 Avenue of the Americas, New York, NY 10020.

Visit our Web site at www.twbookmark.com
For information on Time Warner Trade Publishing's online publishing program, visit www.ipublish.com

An AOL Time Warner Company

The Mysterious Press name and logo are registered trademarks of Warner Books, Inc.

Printed in the United States of America

First Printing: November 2001

10 9 8 7 6 5 4 3 2 1
Library of Congress Cataloging-in-Publication Data

Stark, Richard
    Firebreak / Richard Stark.
        p. cm.
    ISBN 0-89296-711-0
    1. Parker (Fictitious character)—Fiction. 2. Art thefts—Fiction.
3. Criminals—Fiction. 4. Montana—Fiction. I. Title.

PS3573.E9 F55 2001
813'.54—dc21   2001023373

For Bill Malloy, who read it first

ONE

1

When the phone rang, Parker was in the garage, killing a man. His knees pressed down on the interloper's back, his hands were clasped around his forehead. He heard the phone ring, distantly, in the house, as he jerked his forearms back; heard the neck snap; heard the phone's second ring, cut off, as Claire answered, somewhere in the house.

No time to do anything with the body now. Parker stood and was entering the kitchen from the garage when Claire came in the other way, carrying the cordless. "He says his name is Elkins," she told him.

He knew the name. This would have nothing to do with the interloper. Taking the cordless, he said, "I'll have to go out for a while." Then, moving into the dining room, where the windows looked away from the lake, out toward the woods where the stranger had come from, he said, "Frank?"

It was the familiar voice: "Ralph and I maybe have something."

Parker didn't see anybody else out there, among the trees, where the first one had come crouching, a long-barreled pistol held against his right leg; long because it was equipped with a silencer. Parker had first seen him from this room, tracked his moves, met him when he came in the side window of the garage. Into the phone, still watching the empty woods, he said, "You want to call me, or do I call you?"

"Either way."

Parker gave him the number, backward, of the pay phone at the gas station a few miles from here, then said, "Give me a little while, I've got something to finish up here." The woods stayed empty. Now, early October, the trees were still fully leafed out, though starting to turn, and too dense for him to see as far as the road.

Elkins said, "Eleven?"

"Good."

Parker hung up, went back to the garage, and searched the body. There were a wallet, a Ford automobile key, a motel room key, a five-inch spring knife, a pair of sunglasses, and a Zippo lighter but no cigarettes. A green and yellow football helmet was embossed on the lighter. The wallet contained a little over four hundred dollars in cash, three credit cards made out to Viktor Charov, and an Illinois driver's license to the same name, with an address in Chicago. The picture on the license was the dead man: fiftyish, rail-thin, almost bald with a little pepper-and-salt hair around the edges, eyes that didn't show much.

Parker kept the wallet and the key to the Ford, put the rest back, and stuffed the body into the trunk of the Lexus. Then he crossed to the button next to the kitchen entry that operated the overhead garage door, but first slid open the concealed wood panel above it and took out the S&W Chiefs Special .38 he kept stashed there. Finally, then, he pushed the button, and kept the bulk of the Lexus between himself and the steadily lifting view outside.

Nothing. Nobody.

Hand and revolver at his side, like the other one, he stepped out to the chill sunshine and walked at a normal pace out the driveway to the road, watching the woods on both sides. There were other houses around the lake, none of them visible from here, most of them already closed for the winter. Parker and Claire were among the few year-rounders, and they always moved somewhere else in the summer, when the city people came out to their "cottages" and the powerboats snarled on the lake.

The road was empty. Down to the right, fifty paces, stood a red Ford Taurus. Parker walked toward it and saw the rental company sticker on the bumper.

The dead man's Ford key fit the Taurus. Parker started it, swung it around, and drove back to the house, turning in at the driveway where the mailbox read WILLIS.

The garage door stood open, as he'd left it, the dark

green Lexus bulking in there. Parker swung the Ford around, backed it to the open doorway, and switched off the engine. Getting out, he put the S&W away, then took a pair of rubber gloves from the Lexus glove compartment and slipped them on. Then he opened both trunks and moved the body into the Ford.

The dead man's gun was a .357 Colt Trooper with a ribbed silencer clamped behind the front sight. Snapping off the silencer, he put both pieces in a drawer of the worktable under the window where the stranger had come in, his balance between table and floor thrown off just long enough.

On the way into the house, he shut the garage door, its wood sections sliding down between the Lexus and the Ford. He went through the kitchen and found Claire in the living room, reading a magazine. She looked up when he came in, and he said, "I'd like you to pick me up, at the Mobil station, five after eleven."

"Fine. Can we go somewhere for lunch?"

"You pick it."

"I will. See you then." She didn't ask, and wouldn't ask, not because he didn't want to tell her but because she didn't want to know. Whatever happened out of her sight didn't happen.

Three miles beyond the Mobil station a dirt road led off to an old gravel quarry, used up half a century ago by the road building after World War II. The chain-link fences surrounding the property were old and staggering, a joke, and the Warning and No Trespassing and Posted signs had been so painted over by hunters and lovers down the years that they looked like Pollocks.

Parker drove through a broken-down part of the fence and stopped, in neutral, engine on, all the windows open, at the lip, where the stony trash-laden ground ran steeply down to the water that had filled the excavation as soon as work had stopped. Getting out, shutting the door, he moved around behind the Ford and leaned on it. As soon as it started to move, he stepped back, peeling off the gloves, putting them in his pocket, and watched the car bounce down through the rocks and trash till it shoved into the water, making a modest ripple in front of itself that opened out and out and didn't stop till it pinged against the stone at the far side of the quarry. As the car angled down, the black water all around it became suddenly crystal clear as it splashed in through the open windows. The roof sank, a few bubbles appeared, and then only the ripple, going out, slowly fading.

He walked back along the state road to the Mobil station, getting there five minutes early, and leaned against the pay phone, at the outer corner of the station property. A couple of customers came in for gas, paying no attention to him. It was self-serve, so the attendant stayed inside his convenience store.

At two minutes after eleven, the phone rang. Parker stepped around into the booth, which was just a three-sided metal box on a stick, picked up the receiver, and said, "Yes."

It was Elkins' voice: "So I guess you're not too busy right now."

"Not busy," Parker agreed.

"I got something," Elkins told him. "Me and Ralph." Meaning the partner he almost always paired with, Ralph Wiss. "But it won't be easy."

They were never easy. Parker said, "Where?"

"Soon. Sooner the better. We got a deadline."

That was different. Usually, the jobs didn't come with deadlines. Parker said, "You want me to listen?"

"Not now," Elkins said. He sounded surprised.

"I didn't mean now."

"Oh. Yeah, if you wanna take a drive."

"Where?"

"Lake Placid."

A resort in northern New York State, close to Canada. If that was the spot for the meet, it wouldn't be the spot for the work. Parker said, "When?"

"Three tomorrow afternoon?"

Meaning a seven-hour drive, from eight in the morning. Parker said, "Because of your deadline."

"And we don't like to keep things hang around."

Which was true. The longer a job was in the planning, the more chance the law would get wind of it. Parker said, "I can make that," and the Lexus turned in from the road.

"At the Holiday Inn," Elkins said. "Unless you know anybody up that way."

"I do," Parker said. "Viktor Charov. You want to

meet there?" Claire swung the Lexus around to put the passenger door next to the phone.

"Viktor Charov," Elkins said. "I'll find him."

"Good," Parker said.

2

I made a reservation yesterday," Parker said. "Viktor Charov."

"Oh, yes, sir," the clerk said. "I think we even have a message for you."

"Good."

He checked in, writing different things on the form, signing Charov's small crabbed signature, while she went to get the message from the cubbyholes. It was in a Holiday Inn envelope, with VICTOR CHAROV hand-printed on the front. While she ran Charov's credit card, he opened the envelope, opened the Holiday Inn stationery inside, and read "342."

He pocketed the message, signed the credit card form, and accepted the key card for 219. He left his bag in that room, then went down the hall to 243 and knocked on the door. He waited a minute, the hall empty, and then Frank Elkins opened it. A rangy, fortyish man, he looked like a carpenter or a bus driver, except for his eyes, which never stopped moving. He looked at Parker, past him, around him, at him, and said, "Right on time."

"Yes," Parker said, and stepped in, looking at the other two in the room while Elkins shut the door.

The one he knew was Elkins' partner, Ralph Wiss, a safe and lock man, small and narrow, with sharp nose and chin. The other one didn't look right in this company. Early thirties, medium build gone a bit to flab, he had a round neat head, thinning sandy hair, and a pale forgettable face except for prominent horn-rim eyeglasses. While Parker and the other two were dressed in dark trousers and shirts and jackets, this one was in a blue button-down shirt with pens in a pen protector in the pocket, plus uncreased chinos and bulky elaborate sneakers. Parker looked at this one, waiting for an explanation, and Elkins came past him to say, "You know Ralph. This is Larry Lloyd. Larry, this is Parker."

"Hi," Lloyd said, coming forward with a nervous smile to shake hands. "I knew Otto Mainzer on the inside," he added, as though to prove his bona fides. "I think you used to know him, too."

This was a double surprise. First, that somebody who looked like this had ever been in prison, and second that Mainzer still was. Parker said, "Otto isn't out?"

"He hit a guard," Lloyd said, and shrugged. The

nervous grin seemed to be a part of him, like his hair. "He hit people a lot, but then he hit a guard."

"Sounds like Otto," Parker said.

"Larry's our electronics man," Elkins said, as Wiss said, "We're having bourbon."

"Sure," Parker said, and turned to Elkins: "You need an electronics man?"

"Let me tell you the story."

This was the living room of a suite, doors open in both side walls leading to the bedrooms, the picture window looking out over the steeply downhill town of Lake Placid, away from the lake. Coming in, Parker had driven past the two ski jump towers left from the Olympics, and even without snow the town out there had the look of a mountain winter resort, with touches of Alpine architecture scattered among the American logos.

When they sat around the coffee table, Parker noticed that Lloyd's glass contained water. He looked away from it, and Elkins said, "Ralph subscribes to the shelter magazines, you know what I mean."

Parker nodded. He knew other people who did that, bought the glossy architecture magazines because mostly they were color pictures of the insides of rich people's houses. Here's the layout, here are the doors and windows, here's what's worth taking. Parker wasn't usually interested in looting living rooms, but would go to places like banks, where the value was more concentrated; still, he knew what the shelter magazines were for. "He found a house," he said.

Wiss laughed. "I found the palace," he said, "Aladdin went to with his lamp."

"What it is," Elkins said, "there's this billionaire, one of the dot-com people, computer whizzes, made all this money all at once, yesterday he's a geek, today he's giving polo fields to his alma mater."

"He was always a good boy," Wiss said.

Parker said, "This guy got a name?"

"Paxton Marino," Elkins said.

Wiss said, "If you want to call that a name."

"You won't have heard of him," Elkins said. "He got into the dot-com thing early, made his billions, got out, now he's having fun. And he built a house. Actually, I think, so far he's built about eight houses, here and there around the world, but this one's in Montana."

"His hunting lodge," Wiss said, and laughed again.

"Twenty-one rooms," Elkins said, "fifteen baths, separate house down the hill for the staff."

"Isolated," Wiss said.

"He used to go there more often," Elkins said, "maybe five or six separate weeks around the year, but now with all his other stuff it's down to just once a year, ten days, in elk season, believe it or not."

Wiss said, "His elk hunting license is in Canada, but his land extends over the border, he's built a road up into the woods."

Parker said, "You said hunting lodge. What's there gonna be in a hunting lodge?"

"Gold," Wiss said, with a big smile.

"This isn't a hunting lodge," Elkins added, "like a hunting lodge. Antlers and stone fireplaces and all that shit. Ralph's right, it's like a palace."

"Full of gold," Wiss repeated.

"The guy loves gold," Elkins explained. "Every bathroom is gold. Fifteen baths. Not just the faucets, the whole sink."

"The toilets," Wiss said.

Elkins said, "This is where the guy is in his life, him and his friends shit on gold."

"Gold is heavy," Parker pointed out.

"Not a problem," Wiss said.

"We look to see," Elkins said, "when isn't it elk season. Ralph and me and two other guys, we go up there with two trucks and a forklift, like the kind they use in warehouses. You know, slide it under the pallet, move a ton of crap."

"I did blowups of some of the pictures," Wiss said, "I worked out the alarm system. We went up there, and we watched, freezing our asses off, and a guy from the staff house comes up once a day, in the afternoon, goes through the house, turns on and off every light, flushes every toilet, drives back down the hill. That's it. They figure the road's private, and it goes up past the staff house, and they got motion sensors in the house, signal both the staff and the state cops, so they're covered."

"So we went in," Wiss said. "We got rid of all the alarm shit, and then the first thing we wanna do is turn off the water, because we're gonna be ripping out a lotta toilets."

"And sinks," Elkins added.

"So we go into the basement," Wiss went on, "and Frank noticed it, I didn't."

"I was standing right," Elkins explained, "for the light."

"The big main room in the basement," Wiss said, "is wall-to-wall carpet, and there's rooms off it, wine collection, VCR tape collection, one room's like a whole sporting-goods store. But Frank noticed, there's a pale line in the carpet, a lotta travel along one line, the nap's like a little beaten down there, and it goes straight to a blank wall."

"There's something inside there," Parker said.

"This is a guy," Wiss said, "puts his gold in the bathrooms. What's he *hide*?"

"Not the porn," Elkins said, "that's out, too, where you can see it."

Parker said, "So you broke in."

"Hell to find the door," Wiss told him. "We really had to pry shit out of that wall. But then there it was."

"An art gallery," Elkins said.

"Three rooms," Wiss said, "pretty good-size rooms."

"Oil paintings," Elkins said. "What you call Old Masters, famous European artists. Rembrandt, Titian, like that."

"We're walking through," Wiss said, "we're wondering, is this a better deal than the gold toilets, it's a lot lighter, it's worth who knows how much, three rooms of Old Masters."

"And then we recognize three of them," Elkins said.

"That's right," Wiss said, with another laugh. "All of a sudden, here's three old friends."

"We stole them once before," Elkins explained.

"Three years ago," Wiss said, "out of a museum in Houston, a special European show, traveling through."

"Very famous paintings," Elkins said. "Nobody could try to sell them."

"Our fence," Wiss said, "had a guy, wanted just those particular three pictures, and would pay a *lot* for them. And it was a guarantee, he'd never peddle them, or deal with insurance companies, or show them anywhere, but just keep them hidden, a little secret stash for him and his friends."

"Bingo," Elkins said.

3

I wasn't there for that part of it," Lloyd said, and sipped his water. This was the first thing he'd said since Elkins and Wiss had started their story.

Grinning, Wiss said, "Larry, you'd be back inside if you were there for that part of it."

"And we nearly wound up inside, too," Elkins added.

Parker said, "Just to break in on this for a second. Larry, why were you inside?"

Lloyd looked sheepish. "Well, mostly," he said, "attempted murder. The rest they folded into it, the grand theft auto, the embezzling, all of that." He shrugged, and offered that nervous smile, and said, "One little movement becomes fifteen, twenty separate crimes."

"They like to slice and dice, the law," Wiss said.

"They slice what you did into little pieces, so they can dice *you.*"

Parker said to Lloyd, "You're on parole?"

"Yes, I am."

Nodding at Elkins and Wiss, Parker said, "How many crimes you committing right now, in this room?"

"About twelve," Lloyd said. "When I came across the line from Massachusetts, I was already in violation."

"So now you're on the run?"

"Not me," Lloyd said. "Right after this meeting, I'm going home."

Wiss grinned at Lloyd like a fond parent, and said to Parker, "They put an electronic keeper on him."

With a modest shrug, Lloyd said, "It believes I'm in a library in Pittsfield right now."

Parker said, "That's right, you're the electronics man." Looking at Elkins, he said, "And so's Paxton Marino."

"That's it," Elkins agreed. "We broke into that private art gallery of his, and we set off a whole different alarm system we didn't know anything about."

Wiss said, "Fiber-optic lines in conduit in concrete, *under* the house, underground down the hill, separate power source, separate alarms, unreachable."

"You can turn off everything in that house," Elkins said, "shut down the electricity halfway down the road, that art gallery's still humming."

"Which we didn't know," Wiss pointed out, "till our partners yelled down to us there's red flashers coming."

"If they'd of come up quiet," Elkins said, "they'd of got us."

Wiss said, "They got our partners."

Parker said, "How'd that work?"

Elkins explained, "They thought they could outrun them downslope to the intersection. We didn't. We took the other truck and drove up into the woods, along that road he built."

"That doesn't go anywhere," Wiss added.

Elkins shook his head. "Only to the elk."

Wiss said, "We came to the end of the road, and fuck it, we kept driving."

"Until we crashed the truck," Elkins said. "From there on, we walked."

"Freezing our asses off," Wiss said.

"Come on, Ralph," Elkins objected, "it wasn't *that* cold. It was September."

"It was September in Canada," Wiss said.

"Anyway," Elkins said, "we didn't want to walk in circles there in the dark, so we just got away from the truck and hunkered down and waited for morning."

"They never did come up," Wiss said. "Not that night."

"We figure," Elkins said, "at first they thought it was just the two guys they caught, and the one truck. So that worked out for us. But we still had to walk north, away from there, all the next day, through this forest, until we found a road in Canada."

"So you got out," Parker said, "but your partners got nabbed."

"Right now, they're out on humongous bail," Elkins
said. "Their lawyers are dickering with the prosecutors."

"About what?"

"Us," Wiss said.

"They blame us for what happened," Elkins explained. "If we'd just gone in and took the gold, plan
A, we wouldn't of tripped those extra alarms."

Parker said, "So what do they want?"

"Us to go back," Elkins said. "*Get* the Old Masters
this time, divvy with them."

"Why?"

"Because they wanna jump bail, and it's their families' money and houses and stuff, and the job would
cover it."

"Or?"

"Or they turn us up for a better deal and they don't
jump bail."

"Not good for us," Wiss pointed out. "Frank and
me, we're family men, we got roots, we can't live on
the run."

"*Or* in the pen," Elkins said.

Parker said, "And this has to be done right away."

"Before they get a trial date."

Wiss said, "And that brings us to Larry."

Standing, Elkins said, "Larry, you explain it, I made
myself thirsty," and he went off to get the bourbon bottle.

Lloyd said, "When I got out, Frank and Ralph were
among the people I was told to get in touch with by

friends I made on the inside. That was four months ago. I don't think they took me seriously at that time."

"We didn't have a use for your talents at that time," Wiss corrected him.

"Whatever." Lloyd nodded at Wiss, then said to Parker, "What they did at Marino's house, essentially, was make a firebreak, the small fire you set in front of the big fire to steal its fuel and keep it from coming on. By breaking in once, but not managing to come out with anything, they've told Marino and his people what the weaknesses are in the system. It will have been upgraded by now, but there's no telling exactly how. I do know the original structure used the Internet as part of the alarm system, but apparently they didn't have cameras installed in there."

"Lucky for us," Wiss commented.

"Probably what it is," Lloyd said, "if this art collection really does contain that many well-known stolen artworks, Marino doesn't *want* to train a surveillance camera on it. But he might decide now to go to infrared. We can't tell from out here what he'll decide to do. The only thing we know for sure is, whatever he decides, he'll have the money to pay for it."

Elkins was in his chair again, the bottle on the coffee table. Parker said to him, "What's your idea?"

"We're looking for one," Elkins said. "Once we're in, Larry can deal with the science-fiction shit, and Ralph can handle the normal locks and barriers and all that, and I'm good at the logistics, getting the materiel we need, getting everything out."

Wiss said, "We were thinking, this time, maybe we'd come *in* from the north."

Elkins said, "I got Saskatchewan maps, Montana maps, surveyors' maps, all that stuff. There used to be a lot of logging up there, still is some, there's little roads and trails all over the hills up there."

"None of which we found, unfortunately," Wiss added, "for most of a day."

"But now we know where they are," Elkins said, "from the maps. And we can get *to* the place from that side. But we still need a solid way to get in."

Parker said, "I don't like traveling a lot around Canada. Too many ID problems."

Wiss said, "No, we don't need to go through Saskatchewan, we can still be based in Great Falls like last time, and drive up eighty-seven through Havre. It's when we're in the wilderness up there, we may cross-border a little."

Parker said, "You don't have an easier way to get these guys their money?"

"If you know of something," Wiss said, "Frank and me'll listen."

"No, I've got nothing," Parker said. "A little thing I have to do, but there's no money in it."

"This one isn't easy," Elkins said, "but they never are. It's worth your while, Parker, if you come in on this."

"Worth your while, too."

"We know that," Wiss said, "that's why Frank called you."

Parker considered. He had nothing else, he didn't know who had hired the hit man, Charov, he didn't know what complications that could lead to, but it looked as though he and Claire should stay away from the house for a while. He said, "You cover my expenses."

"Done," Elkins said.

"And I don't pay you back out of my piece."

"No, I understand that."

"I gotta deal with a different problem tomorrow," Parker said. "Where and when do you want to meet?"

"The Muir, in Great Falls, next Monday," Elkins said. "You'll still be Lynch?"

"Yes." Looking at Lloyd, he said, "You're gonna be in Montana, your electronic gizmo is still gonna think you're in a library in Massachusetts?"

Lloyd laughed, with real pleasure, like a kid. "That's what makes it fun," he said.

4

Charov's place was a furnished apartment on Chicago's South Side, near Marquette Park. It was a sprawling dark brick building with a transient air to it, as though no one had ever planned to stay there long. Half the mailboxes and doorbells were unmarked, and many of the rest were handwritten on torn-off pieces of cardboard or strips of masking tape. Two bicycles in the clean but bleak front vestibule were heavily chained to vertical metal pipes, heat risers.

Charov's name was among the missing on mailboxes and doorbells, and Parker had no way to know which apartment was his. He found the super's apartment at the ground floor rear, beyond the staircase, and the second time he knocked the door was opened by a fiftyish very short stout woman in yellow tank top and jeans, barefoot. A lit cigarette was in the corner of her mouth, an unlit one behind her left ear. In her free hand she held a copy of the *Star*. She gave Parker a sharp suspicious look, decided he was neither a tenant nor a cop, and said, "Yeah?"

"My brother Viktor's supposed to meet me at the airport," Parker told her. He acted bewildered, starting to be worried, not very smart. He held his airline ticket up to show her, saying, "See? I flew in from Albany, Viktor's supposed to meet me, he never showed up."

She frowned at the ticket he was waving. "Whado I care?"

"He lives here! Viktor Charov!"

"Oh," she said, nodding, recognizing the name. "Sure, that's right."

"I had to take a cab in from O'Hare," Parker told her. "Twenty-three bucks! Viktor never showed up."

"Maybe he's stuck in traffic," she said.

"Maybe it's his heart," Parker suggested. "He had heart trouble once, maybe he's sick."

She made an effort to act concerned. "Did you try calling him?"

"No answer," he told her. "Come with me, open the door, let's see if he's there."

She looked at her newspaper, frowning, not wanting to have to move out of her nest. "My husband's upstairs fixing a sink," she said.

"We'll just take a look," Parker told her, "make sure he isn't there, hurt or something."

She sighed, feeling sorry for herself. "All right, just a minute."

She didn't ask him in, but shut the door, and he waited in the hall until she came out, now wearing sneakers and a lavender cardigan sweater. The cigarette was gone from her mouth, but the other one was still behind her ear. "Come on," she said.

The elevator was old and slow and a little too small. It creaked up the shaft to the fourth floor, and she led the way down a clean gray hall to the third dark brown metal door on the left. "L" it said. The slot for a tenant to slip a card into with his name on it was blank.

She unlocked the door, leaned in, called, "Mr. Charov?" She listened, then turned back, shaking her head. "He isn't here."

"We gotta look," Parker said.

She frowned at him, irritated at how much of her time he was using, and shrugged. "But we don't touch nothing," she said.

They entered a narrow short foyer with a closet on the left, then a small living room with two windows in the opposite wall overlooking the street, and doors open in both side walls. The one on the left led to the bedroom, with a bathroom beyond it, and to the right was the kitchen. All was anonymously furnished by the landlord, with a few stray indications of Charov's tenancy. The rooms were empty.

"Like I said," the woman told him. "Stuck in traffic."

"I'll wait for him," Parker said.

"You can't wait in here," the woman said. "I know, I know, you're his brother, but I still can't let you wait in here. The weather's nice, you can sit on the stoop."

"Fine," Parker said.

They went back to the hall door, Parker first. He held the door open for her to go through, and on the way out pushed the button that unlocked the door.

Guns were stashed in every room, small lightweight .22s, meant to end the argument right away in small rooms like these. They were snapped into clips under chairs, behind the toilet, under the bed.

Twelve thousand dollars in twenties and fifties was rolled into an orange juice concentrate can in the freezer. Inside the lining of the suitcase in the bedroom closet were Russian, Ukraine, and Belarus passports with Charov's face but other names. Under the socks in the top dresser drawer was a manila envelope that had once been mailed to Charov at this address, with a printed return address of Cosmopolitan Beverages in Bayonne, New Jersey; whatever it had originally held, Charov had been using it to hold his papers. There was an American green card, plus documents describing him as an executive employed by Cosmopolitan Beverages, an importer of Russian liquors. Also in the envelope was an open-date Aeroflot ticket, first-class, from New York's JFK to Moscow.

Stuck into the edge of the mirror over the dresser were three color snapshots of what had to be Charov's family, back in Moscow; a pleasant plump wife, three teenage sons, and a large brown-black dog that looked like a mix of German shepherd and wolf, all standing

in sunlight in front of a large, comfortable-looking but
not gaudy suburban house.

Beside the bed was a telephone with answering machine, its red light blinking the news that it contained
two messages. Parker pushed play and the first message was a guttural voice leaving a brisk statement in
what was probably Russian. The second, in English,
was from somebody who sounded hesitant, nervous, a
little scared: "Charov? Are you there? I thought I'd
hear from you by now. Everything's okay, isn't it? I'm
ready with the money. Just call me. Let me know how
things went."

The customer. Too cagy or nervous to leave his
name.

Parker played the message again. The voice was almost familiar, almost. He played it a third time, but he
wasn't going to get it. Too far in the past, or too little
known.

Next to the answering machine was a notepad, with
three items written on it:

п.Брок

М.Розенштєрн

WILLIS

That last one was in the Roman alphabet because
that's what it would say on the mailbox outside
Parker's house on the lake. It was the landmark
Charov would have looked for.

And the first two names, if they were names? They

looked like names. Was one of them the nervous voice on the answering machine? On the phone, here, had Charov written the names of his new employers and the target?

Parker left the guns where they were. He took with him the money, the passports, the manila envelope with everything in it, and the notepad with the names.

5

Cosmopolitan Beverages."

"Viktor Charov, please," Parker said.

"I'm sorry, what?"

"Viktor Charov."

"No, sir, I'm sorry, there's no one here by that name."

"Oh, is he in Moscow?"

"No, sir, we don't— What was that name again?"

"Viktor Charov," Parker said. "He's a purchasing agent with your outfit. He isn't there?"

"Hold, please."

Parker held. Traffic was light going by the gas station, the same one where he'd talked with Elkins. He hadn't been to the house yet, see what was going on there. Claire had moved to a hotel in New York, planned to do some shopping; he'd call her later, after he knew what was going on.

"Ms. Bursar."

"Hello," Parker said. "I'm looking for Viktor Charov."

"Would you spell that name?"

He did, with the *k*, and Ms. Bursar said, "There's no one by that name employed here."

"I'm sure he is," Parker said. "He travels back and forth to Moscow for you people."

"Sir, I am the firm's accountant," Ms. Bursar said. "I write the salary checks, and I have never written a check for anyone named Viktor Charov."

"Well, I got a bum steer then," Parker said. "Sorry about that."

"There are a number of other beverage importers in this area," Ms. Bursar pointed out. "Perhaps he's with one of them."

"Could be," Parker said, and hung up, and went back to the Lexus.

A no-show job, to cover Charov's travels between the two countries and explain his income. Somebody connected with Cosmopolitan was mobbed-up in some way, and could insert this ringer into the company without its accountant knowing he was there.

Which was why, though his "employer" was in a town next to the harbor of New York, Charov's American base had been Chicago. That was much more central for somebody whose actual work might take him anywhere in the country.

For years the hit men came from Italy, know-nothing rural toughs called zips, who spoke no English, came in only to do the job and collect their low pay, and then flew back out again. But that system soon began to break down. Some of the zips refused to go home, some of them got caught and didn't know how to take care of themselves inside the American system, some of them had loyalties in Europe that conflicted with their one-time-only employers in the United States.

It's still better, all in all, to have a contract killer whose home base is far away, in some other land. But it pays to have somebody reliable, educated, useful over the long term. Viktor Charov could come and go as he pleased, cloaked by his "job" at Cosmopolitan Beverages. He could take on whatever private work he wanted, and from time to time the people who'd given him his cover would ask him to do a little something for them.

But the mob wasn't behind the run at Parker. That had been a civilian, that nervous voice on the answering machine in Chicago. It was one of his independent contractor jobs that had run out Charov's string.

No one had been in the house. Parker went through it, slowly, room by room, and all the little signals he'd set there were unsprung.

The civilian employer of Charov would react slowly to the Russian's disappearance. There was time to see if the Montana job was worth the effort. Time to find out what those two names in Cyrillic looked like when they were at home.

Parker phoned the hotel in Manhattan, but Claire was out, as he'd expected. He left a message: "See you in a week or two."

6

The Big Sky Airlines commuter plane took Parker the last leg from Great Falls, Montana, up to Havre, twenty-five miles from Canada. Elkins met him in a rental Jeep Cherokee. "Get your other stuff taken care of?"

"It's waiting for me," Parker said.

They had to go through Havre, small and neat and flat, still a railroad town, surrounded by the mountains. Three peaks of the Bear Paw Mountains, Baldy and Bates and Otis, six to seven thousand feet high, were all within twenty minutes of the center of town.

Route 2, the east-west road, ran along beside the Milk River from here almost a hundred miles to Malta, but their motel, a non-chain operation called Thibadeau View, was just a couple miles east of town, toward Chinook. The motel, a long white one-story wood clapboard building dwarfed by its Indian-motif sign, stood on the left, the north side of the road, with the quick-tumbling Milk River behind it.

It was seven in the evening, local time. The motel didn't have a restaurant, so after Parker put his bag in his room the four of them drove to a place that called itself a family restaurant. They weren't the family the owners had in mind.

Over the meal, Elkins said, "We figure to go up there tonight, take a look at the place. Also, Larry's gotta head back to Massachusetts tomorrow."

Parker looked at Lloyd. "You're gonna commute? Massachusetts to Montana?"

"No, I won't come back after this," Lloyd told him. "I have to get physically close just this once, to find my access, since it isn't a normal site with normal ways in. But after that, I can deal with it from home."

Wiss continued to take an almost paternal pride in Lloyd, saying, "Do you like that, Parker? He's gonna pick the lock over the Web."

"If he misses," Parker said, "we're the ones on the scene. And he's the one with the electronic alibi."

Wiss shook his head. "Larry won't miss," he said.

"I'll be in touch with Ralph through the whole thing," Lloyd explained. "He'll have a portable with him. Whatever's happening there, I'll know about it as soon as you do."

"I'm told there's nothing secure on the Web," Parker said. "Everybody hears everything."

"We're talkin about a chess game," Wiss explained.

"We got it all worked out, openins, gambits, sacrifices. Larry and me both play chess anyway, so it'll be easy."

Parker could imagine circumstances that could make it less than easy. If they had a listener, and if the listener knew chess, and if the listener heard moves that didn't make sense. But it didn't seem to be enough of a problem that he'd want them to look for some other way to talk, back and forth, some different way that might be even less easy and more risky. Having a member of the string that meant to phone in his part was strange, but everybody seemed to think they could make it work, so Parker shrugged and said, "Fine."

"You folks want dessert?" the waitress asked.

They didn't.

In the woods, close to or maybe over the Canadian border, they traveled without lights. Wiss and Elkins both wore infrared goggles, Wiss behind the wheel, Elkins walking out front. Elkins carried a geological survey map and a compass, and kept looking for vehicle-friendly terrain in the direction they wanted to go. Wiss watched Elkins and drove where he walked.

In the backseat, Parker and Lloyd couldn't see a thing, only feel the slow sway and jounce of the Cherokee as it eased forward. There were high clouds, a thin sliver of moon, not enough starshine to make much difference. Here under the trees, without the goggles, everything was black.

After they'd driven awhile in the darkness, Parker said, "Tell me why you were in."

Lloyd's voice, to his left, sounded pained but tired: "I'm trying to forget all that."

"I need you to remember it," Parker told him, "or you can forget me."

"Why? You know Frank and Ralph, don't you?"

"But I don't know you. And I don't go by other people's judgment."

There was a little silence over there, while Lloyd got used to the idea, and then he sighed and said, "I'm not proud of it."

"Most people aren't."

"I mean, I was stupid, I was emotional, I was hasty, I was careless, I was everything I've always prided myself on *not* being."

"When was this?"

Lloyd let out a long breath. "All right," he said. "In engineering school, I partnered with a guy named Brad Grenholz, a brilliant guy, a real innovator. I was always more of the grind, the detail man, the one who tidied up."

"So you made a good team."

"The best. If only—"

Parker waited, and finally Lloyd did another long sigh and said, "When you spend all your imaginative time inside molecules, it makes you nervous. You're very fast, and very jumpy, but you don't think you're fast *enough*, you need to be *more* jumpy, so pretty soon Brad and I were doing a lot of drugs. A lot of drugs.

Liquor, too, but that was to come down. That was our only downer. Everything else we took was uppers. I swear, static electricity ran over our bodies like an electrode."

"Can't last," Parker said.

"It wasn't *supposed* to last. The thing is, we came up with— The two of us came up with, but that was a dispute later, but the two of us came up with a server application that was just *awesome*. Everybody wanted to invest, we had *Brazilians* wanted to invest!"

"Drug money?"

"No! Legit legit! *Bank* money! Venture *capital* money! All of a sudden, barely out of school, we're millionaires! On paper, but still. Millionaires."

"He screwed you," Parker suggested.

"It's that obvious, isn't it," Lloyd agreed, disgusted with himself. "I trusted him, I thought we were a team forever. There had to be contracts, legal papers, deals, all of that, but that wasn't the real stuff, the stuff inside the molecules was the real stuff, and the stuff in our veins. So Brad's sister's husband's brother was our lawyer, but so what, he was *our* lawyer, we all loved each other."

"Until," Parker said.

"Until there was a distribution," Lloyd told him, "and I wasn't part of it. Everything had been going into the business until then, just a little draw for us to live on, but now there was the first distribution, and Brad is on the list, and his sister and her husband are on the list, and the lawyer's *wife* is on the list, but I'm not on the list."

Lloyd was silent. The Cherokee kept creeping around tree trunks and boulders, skirting ravines and too-steep slopes, looking for the road down to Marino's place. Parker waited for Lloyd to calm himself down, silent and invisible over there.

"All right," Lloyd finally said. "Thank you for not pressing me."

"We've got time," Parker said.

"Yes. All right. What I did— I couldn't bring myself to go to Brad, as though I was accusing him, because it had to be a simple fuckup, an explanation somewhere, so I brought it to our office manager, the one in charge of disbursements, and *she* said the list was straight from George. The lawyer, George. I said this can't be right, this is some sort of fuckup, I called George, George told me to look at the papers I'd signed, I was an *employee,* he offered to fax me over copies of everything I'd signed in case I didn't have it all myself, I hung up on him. I thought, Brad can't know about this, this is something George the sleazy lawyer did because he's George the sleazy lawyer, it's a sleazy lawyer thing is all. So I went to see Brad, he had a nice weekend place north of the city—New York, I mean—up in the Shawangunks, good climbing mountains, he'd become a mountaineer by then, and I confronted him, I mean, to the extent I ever confronted anybody, and he was very bland and smooth and of course we were both stoned, we were *always* stoned but functioning, you know, that creative high, and he said I'd never been anything but his assistant from the beginning, he was the genius with the ideas, I was his girl Friday, that's all I was. So I hit him with a laptop, right on the back of the head with a laptop, and threw him off his goddam terrace with the great view of the Gunks, and threw his laptop after him, and I seriously positively wanted to kill him, and thought I had. And I set fire to the house, and I stole his Porsche, and I forged his name to a few checks, and I tried to access the business accounts so I could steal everything, and somewhere in there they caught me."

"You cut a pretty good swath," Parker said.

"I sure did," Lloyd agreed.

"How long were you in?"

"Six years, four months, nine days."

"Not that long, with everything."

"No, well, that's where it turned out I maybe wasn't that stupid, after all," Lloyd said. "I had a couple things come out right for me later on. Like Brad didn't die, for one, which at first I thought was too fucking bad, but then I realized it was a blessing."

"Because it wasn't murder."

"No, because I could rat him out." Lloyd laughed, a harsh sound, and said, "Due to the fact I'd gone in and screwed everything up, made such a mess of the firm, the feds had to come in and take a look around, and it seemed I wasn't the only one Brad was screwing. He wasn't really doing it for the money, he had money, he was doing it to prove he was smarter than everybody else, and that meant *everybody* else, including the government. Embezzling from his own company to avoid taxes on profits, filing false income tax returns, all kinds of shit like that. So, it turned out, maybe Brad was the genius, and I was just the— He was the grasshopper and I was the ant, but when it came to game theory I thought of it first."

There was another little silence. Again Parker waited him out, and this time Lloyd, sounding defiant and embarrassed, said, "He who flips first wins."

"You went state's evidence."

"I traded my best friend Brad for a reduction of sentence." Lloyd giggled, a strange sound. "He won't be out for a few more years."

"Okay," Parker said.

Now the silence returned in the slowly moving Cherokee. Parker was satisfied, felt there was nothing more to say, but a minute later Lloyd asked, "Does that worry you?"

"Does what worry me?"

"That I ratted out Brad."

"You did what you had to do."

"I just don't want you to think, uh . . ."

Parker said, "Don't worry about it."

"All right."

"You won't be in that situation, with me," Parker said.

* * *

Parker gradually became aware of light, off to his right. It was pinkish gray, dim, diffuse, like a false dawn, but narrower. Lloyd said, "Isn't that—?"

"Maybe it's where we're going," Parker said, and up front Wiss cried, "God *damn*! At last!" He spurted the Cherokee forward a few feet, then stopped, his red brake lights shining from behind Parker, brighter than the faint illumination downslope to the right.

They'd earlier switched off the Cherokee's interior lights, so it stayed dark when Elkins climbed in, saying, "Well, we found it. Too far south, though."

"Doesn't matter," Wiss said.

Parker said, "What doesn't matter?"

Elkins told him, "I wanted to come in above the shed, just to look it over, but we can do that on the way back. Marino's got a shed, like a little cabin, up at the top of the road, in case anybody wants to take a leak, have a shower, drink a beer."

"Small, for him," commented Wiss.

"I figured," Elkins said, "if we went there first, we'd get some idea what's changed around here."

Wiss said, "Should we go up there now?"

"No," Parker said. "We're here. I want to see what those lights are."

"So do I," Elkins said.

"Done," Wiss said, and put the Cherokee in gear.

Elkins had taken his goggles off now, but at first Wiss kept them on as he drove, so he could find the road. Soon, though, the light out ahead got stronger,

more amber now than either pink or gray, and he took
the goggles off.

It was strange, almost an underwater feeling, to
drive into the aura of the light, the pine forest be-
coming more solid, the sky now like a roof, black
where the soft light didn't reach.

Just as Parker saw the first floodlight out ahead of
them, Lloyd sharply said, "Stop! Stop here."

They stopped, and all four got out onto the road, a
narrow ribbon of gray concrete barely two lanes wide,
curving up the slope through the forest, angling
around the larger trees. Ahead of them were two
floodlights, mounted atop twenty-foot-high metal
posts. One was about ten feet from the road to the
right, the other an equal distance to the left. Both
lights were aimed away from them, downslope,
through clear plastic mountings that dimmed and dif-
fused them. There was no glare at any point in among
the trees, just a steady low illumination, as though
Marino had given the entire forest a night-light.

Lloyd said, "This is the new perimeter. These fix-
tures will circle the house."

"Hell of a big perimeter," Wiss said.

"But this is the way to do it," Lloyd told him.
"Mounted up there with those lights will be motion
sensors and cameras. If a deer walks through here—"

"Or an elk," Wiss said.

"Anything," Lloyd agreed. "If anything bigger than
a chipmunk goes into the part that's lit up, it'll sound
an alarm down in their security station, in the staff

house. They look at it, they see it's a bear or a fox, they don't worry about it. They see it's a man, they send somebody."

Elkins said, "This is gonna go all around the place? From way out here?"

"Of course," Lloyd told him. "Comes on automatically at dusk, goes off at daybreak. Just the lights go off. The cameras and sensors stay on."

Parker said, "Let's take a look at this staff house."

Elkins said, "Why?"

"Because you've got to take that out first," Parker said, "or you don't have a score."

They walked around the perimeter, another light on a tall pole always ahead of them like a marker, the lights at equal spacings, all aimed inward toward the center, where the main house would be, too far away to see from out here. Which also meant the lights wouldn't bother anybody in the house. But they'd bother anybody trying to *get* in the house.

It was easy walking, mostly downslope, because clearing had been done when this security system had been put in, just a month or two ago. The cables were all buried, and the result was a narrow path through the forest, curving gently from light to light.

Lloyd led the way, Wiss behind him, then Parker, then Elkins, so it was Lloyd who said, quietly, "Here's a road."

The others came up with him. This was the reverse of the road on the other side, where they'd left the car, where the road had come downslope from darkness to continue on into the light, disappearing among the trees. Here the road came down out of the lit forest, went past them, and continued on down into black.

Elkins said, "This is it. Main house up that way, staff house down there."

"I don't see it," Lloyd said.

"It's probably a quarter mile from here," Elkins told him.

"The fun part," Wiss said, "is when we walk all this way back up the mountain."

They walked down the road, leaving the amber light behind them, and as it faded they picked out another light ahead, a yellowish rectangle. "That'll be security, with the light on," Wiss said.

It was, the one lit window in a dark house. Parker said, "Lloyd, why don't I see any protection here?"

"Well, there's nothing valuable here," Lloyd told him. "They're just supposed to keep guard on the main house."

Closer to the yellow rectangle of window, Parker could dimly make out a two-story boxy house with a wide front porch, the kind of building you'd find on a well-to-do side street anywhere in the midwest. Here in a forest on a mountain it had a lost look, as though the people who'd put it up hadn't stopped first to look around at the setting.

Almost four in the morning. It would be day before they got back to the car, mid-morning before they got back to Havre, and then Lloyd had to start taking planes. Parker said, "We need to know how many people they got in there, and what kind of guns."

Wiss said, "Parker, I like to be a sneak thief when I can. You don't think there's any way to bypass this?"

"None," Parker told him.

Lloyd said, "I have to agree with that."

Elkins said, "After all this, do we have a score or not? Parker, what do you think?"

"Maybe," Parker said.

Lloyd had brought with him Wiss's goggles. Now he put them on, saying, "I've got to see where the cables come in."

They walked down past the house, slowly, Lloyd with the goggles leading the way, looking back and forth, bending to study the ground, finally dropping to all fours to crawl over to the house across a recently mowed lawn. He'd found the service box there, where the underground cables came up to be split to bring power and communication to the house. The others stayed back by the road, trying to see what he was doing, keeping watch that he didn't attract attention from anybody inside the house.

He spent ten minutes there, then crawled back, standing when he reached the road. "I can get in," he said.

"The question is," Elkins said, "can we?"

1

ime to go home," Elkins said, "think it over, figure something out."

Saturday morning, their fifth day here, and they were seated around breakfast again at the family restaurant. Wiss said, "Parker? What do you think? There's something there?"

"Your paintings are there," Parker said.

Lloyd had taken the Cherokee with him, to turn in at the airport at Great Falls. The others had rented a pair of nondescript Tauruses, muddy maroon and muddy green, to spend their week learning about the staff and their house.

It had been Parker's job to chart the movements of the staff. The mountains around here were heavily forested in pine, but the lower slopes, where the roads and towns were located, were much more barren and open, expanses of rock or prairie, where a house or a

car or even a man could be seen for miles. That made
it harder to be an unnoticed observer than in a city,
where somebody seated in one car among a thousand
parked vehicles would never attract attention.

So Parker did it the other way. He got a clipboard
and a yellow hard hat and dark blue coveralls and a
plastic-and-tube folding chair and sat beside the gravel
county road and read the Havre *Daily News*. The
muddy green Taurus was parked just to his left, the
turnoff from the county road up toward Marino's
place was off to his right. The last mile or so of the private road was below the forest and steeply down across
a mostly bare shelf of tan boulder, so he could see traffic from there a long way off. Every time any vehicle at
all went by on the county road he made a mark on the
yellow pad on his clipboard. Every time a car went in
or out of the private road, he made more elaborate
and more meaningful marks.

Most of the vehicles past this spot were pickups, and
most of them were repeats. He got a few curious stares
the first day, but by the second he'd been accepted as
just another guy with a cushy job, and by the third he
was part of the landscape.

A few times during the week, he left his post to follow staffers who'd driven away from the house, until
he got a sense of their errands, where and for how
long they went, what they did or didn't do in the outside world. He did a minimum of that kind of trailing,
because he didn't want to become a presence in their
peripheral vision.

At the same time, this week, Wiss and Elkins had been going through back issues of the *Daily News* in the Havre library, and searching records in the county clerk's office, and chatting with locals in diners and bars, and now, Saturday morning over family breakfast, they told one another what they'd come up with: "Staff's all imports," Wiss said. "None of them local."

"The locals could be peeved about that," Elkins added, "if they thought about it, but they don't, much."

"There's eight staff," Parker told them. "Six men and two women. They've got three identical white Chevy Blazers, with Montana plates."

"Leases," Elkins decided.

"Looks like," Parker said. "They get their mail at a post office box in Havre. They don't have anything delivered, they go out and shop, every day."

"So we don't come in like we're bringing the groceries," Wiss said.

Elkins said, "And we're not a pal of theirs from town. They don't mingle with the natives, not at all. Most people think they're snooty, think they're better than anybody else because they work for a billionaire."

"Well, it's a smart setup," Parker said. "They can keep tighter security if their bunch doesn't mingle with anybody else."

"Then they've got good security," Wiss said.

Elkins said, "Parker? What do you think?"

"There's never more than one car away from the place at a time," Parker said. "I guess the idea is, they want to keep the staff up to strength as much as they can."

"Good security again," Wiss commented.

"I looked up that road once," Parker said, "and about a mile up it starts to twist through some pretty thick forest. We wait till they go out, drive up into the forested part, stop on a blind curve, take the Blazer away from them when they come back. Then we can at least get to the house without setting anything off. But once they see we're somebody else, they'll jump to the alarms. The question is, what can Lloyd do, back in Massachusetts, to keep those alarms from getting off the property?"

"We'll ask him," Elkins said.

8

little after seven that morning, when it would be nine A.M. in New York, Parker phoned Claire at the hotel. She should still be in the room, finishing her coffee, putting on her face.

She was. "I'm glad you called," she said, and he could hear the tension in her voice.

"Something happened?"

"I called Louise," she said, Louise being the woman who cleaned the house by the lake every Thursday. "I called her yesterday, to make sure everything was all right, and she said the lock was broken on the lakeside door."

"Nobody there?"

"Not when she was there, not that she noticed. And it didn't seem to her anything had been taken."

Or left, Parker thought. That was the more important question. Had anything been left there, maybe to blow up, or maybe to signal people waiting. He said, "I was calling to say I'm coming back east, I'd see you in the city, we could have dinner."

"I'd like that."

"But I think I better look at the house first, then call you again."

"All right. Today?"

"I'm gonna be on too many planes today," he said. "I'll call you tomorrow."

"All right."

"The other thing I wanted," he said. "In the city, see if you can find somebody who reads Cyrillic."

"You mean like Russian?"

"Russian. Yes."

9

Once, some years ago, there had been people inside Claire's house that Parker hadn't wanted there, and he'd come in that time at night, in a rowboat taken from another house on the opposite side of the lake, guided by the lights gleaming from houses along the shore. He did the same now, but later, three in the morning, no light visible from any of the houses around him. That other time he'd come across from the far side of the lake, but tonight he started looking for a boat about a quarter mile east of Claire's house, out near the state road.

All the houses along here were shut for the winter. The first two had no boats that he could find, but the third came with a boathouse, like Claire's, and beside it on a concrete dock a small fiberglass dinghy lay face-down. When he rolled it over, its oars were on the concrete beneath it. He put the boat in the water, took one oar to use as a paddle, sat in the boat facing front, as though it were a canoe, and started along the shore-line.

Farther out, starshine defined the water, but this close to shore he was shadowed by the surrounding trees and hills. The houses were hard to tell apart in darkness this complete. It would be the boathouse he'd recognize, not the house itself.

He slid through the water, almost completely silent, the faint whisperings of boat and oar blended into the cool silence of the night. Soon the boathouse was a blacker black ahead of him, blocky, looming. He shipped the oar, let the boat coast forward, then leaned out with one palm to fend off from the corner of the boathouse, keeping the boat clear. Hands along the rough wall of the boathouse on his right, he eased around to the wooden dock, and stopped it there before it could clatter against the concrete patio.

His pistol was in his inside jacket pocket. He put it on the dock in darkness in front of him, at chest height, then stood, leaned forward, went from standing in the boat to kneeling on the dock, the boat shying backward away from him, turning lazily back out toward the lake. He held the pistol, both knees and one palm on the dock, and looked toward the house.

Nothing. Pitch black, under its surrounding trees. The trees were tall and skinny on this side, sparsely placed between house and lake. He moved forward cautiously, left hand out so he wouldn't run into one

of those trees, and eventually came to the screened
porch. The door there opened without a sound.

It was the inner door that had been broken into,
from what Claire had said, and it wouldn't have been
fixed yet. Parker crossed to it, and felt the broken
glass, then eased open the door and stepped inside.

The next hour was slow and careful. Parker moved
as though the house were foreign to him and full of
enemies. He searched for people, for booby traps, for
signs of the interlopers. But at the end of it, there was
no one and nothing here.

The electricity was turned off, and he left it like
that. He went to the living room, sat on the sofa there,
and from time to time dozed until dawn, then got up
and made another very slow circuit through the
house, this time touching nothing, looking at everything.

They hadn't searched the place. They hadn't taken
anything. The only sign they'd been here was the broken glass on the lakeside door.

They'd had a reason to come. If not to take anything, then to leave something.

Yes. Full daylight, and at last he saw it. Above the
main door into the living room from outside, in from
the front of the house toward the road, a narrow
brown hair now dangled down from the top of the
frame. If he were to open that door, it would brush the
hair slightly.

Parker got a chair from the dining room, put it
against the wall a few feet to the right of the door, and

stood on it. Resting atop the door frame was what looked like a very small jeweler's loupe, dulled black metal, round, with a flat non-reflecting glass front. The hair drooped down from that.

A radio camera. If anyone came in that front door, the primary entrance to the house, the hair would move, and the camera would switch on, to broadcast the scene in this living room to its base.

How far would the base be from here? They'd want to be close enough to act, far enough away to be out of sight.

And there'd be a second camera, too, in the garage, in case he were to come in that way. He didn't need to look for it, he knew it was there. Or maybe not even a camera out there, but merely something to tell them when the electric garage door opener had been oper-ated.

Parker put the chair back in the dining room, walked to the screened-in porch, looked out at the lake. Last night's rowboat floated way out there, turn-ing slowly. In crisp fall sunlight, it was vermilion. All the houses he could see were blank-faced, closed for the season.

They could be in any house around the lake. He didn't have the time to search the whole area, and he couldn't cover all that territory without being seen.

Would they come here sometimes, check on the house, on the camera? He didn't want to leave here during daylight, so he went to the kitchen, where he could see the lake and the living room, and waited.

The refrigerator was turned off, door open, but there was dry food in the pantry. He ate, and waited, and no one appeared, and after dark he went out through the screen porch and walked down other people's yards to where he'd left the car.

For now, they could have the house.

10

They had a late dinner, and a good night together, and in the morning breakfast in the room, during which Claire said, "I found a woman who reads Russian. Well, she is Russian."

"Good."

"She's a partner at a furrier in midtown."

"Not one I ever visited, I hope," he said.

She laughed, saying, "No, I'm sure it's all right. She came over from Russia since the breakup, it's a big family in the fur business over there, sable exporting, they decided to get into this end of the trade three years ago."

"You're buying something from her," Parker suggested.

"Of course." Claire shrugged. "Why else would she talk to me?"

*   *   *

Madame Irina was a short pouter pigeon of a woman, in a tight black pantsuit and cotton boll white hair. A pair of harlequin glasses that hung from a gold chain around her neck rested on the shelf of her chest. Her black slippers whispered on the thick black wool of the carpet.

The room was smallish, luxuriously Spartan, with neutral gray walls and a low white ceiling. Low maroon armchairs and sofas made three conversation areas around oval glass coffee tables on which glossy magazines were carefully arranged, like a line of shingles on a roof, as though this were the waiting room for an interplanetary cruise line. Three very tall mannequins in corners, with faces of foreign disdain, wore rich long fur coats.

To the right, a plate-glass window showed an efficient cream office with four employees, all of whom kept glancing this way. The glass would be bulletproof. The valuable stock would be beyond the other door, gray, almost invisible, set into the wall opposite the entrance.

The entrance itself, here on the third floor of this building on Madison Avenue, was a simple airlock-style. They had come out of the elevator, to be eye-balled by the people in the office, who had a second plate-glass window on that side for the purpose. Claire had spoken to a microphone, a polite metallic voice had said, "Of course, Mrs. Willis, come in," and the buzzer had sounded, letting them through a windowed door into a square gray cubicle with another windowed door straight ahead. The door behind them had gently but forcefully snicked itself shut, as Madame Irina had come smiling across the showroom, moving very like a pouter pigeon who has decided, as a whim, to walk just for today.

Parker was certain this inner door wouldn't be openable if he were to keep the first one from shutting, which he didn't do. Madame Irina let them in, door number two shut itself behind them, and here they were.

Parker wasn't here for work, but his response was automatic. He saw it would take two men and a woman to do the job, and he thought Noelle Kay Braselle would do the woman very well. Of course, now that he'd been here with Claire, neither of the men could be him. It was just an instinctive reaction.

"Madame Irina, my husband Charles."

"How do you do, Mr. Charles." Her accent was lilting, seeming more French than Russian. In fact, she wasn't the Russian he'd expected. Her manner was coolly highbred, as though the entire Bolshevik interlude had been no more than unpleasant weekend guests who'd overstayed their welcome. The Russia she came from still had czars.

There was a little discussion between the two women about the three coats Claire had decided to choose among, and then Madame Irina made a murmuring phone call while standing at her gray plastic block desk. Hanging up the gray receiver, she said,

"They'll bring them right out. And Mr. Charles has some names for me to look at?"

"Yes, show them, Charles."

The story was that Charles Willis, a shoe manufacturer with a strong export business, had been told indirectly of a couple of Americans who might be useful in helping him expand his business into the western segments of the old Soviet Union. Unfortunately, the origin of the tip was a Russian who only spoke Russian and only used Cyrillic, so Charles Willis couldn't read the names and therefore didn't know if these were people he already knew or would find it useful to look up. Fortunately, Charles Willis's business was profitable enough so that his wife was buying fur coats from Madame Irina, who could be very helpful in translating these two names.

All of that had been explained by Claire on her previous visit, so all Parker had to do now was take from his jacket pocket the slip of paper with the names on it and hand it over, just as the near-invisible door at the back of the room opened and three models strutted in, wearing the coats.

It was now Parker's job to turn away from Madame Irina and look with interest at the coats, while the models turned and stepped in front of Claire, smiling in a blank way at her, not acknowledging the existence of the husband for a second.

"That one's too dark," she decided.

"If you say so."

"Charles? Do you think this one's too long?"

"Try it on yourself," he said.

"You're right."

The model swirled out of the coat, showing the plain black spaghetti-strap dress beneath, and helped Claire put it on, gesturing toward the full-length mirror on the side wall, as Madame Irina said, "Yes, Mr. Charles, these are Americans."

He gave her the kind of attention Claire was giving the coats. "Which Americans?"

She held the sheet up to show him.

п.Брок
М.Роэенwтєрh

"This first one," she said, touching it, "is the initial P. Then the last name is B-R-O-K. But I think here it would be B-R-O-C-K."

Brock. Paul Brock. Parker had thought he'd never hear from Paul Brock again. The last time he'd seen the man, Parker had shot him and he lay on his back, unable to move, moaning for an ambulance, at the foot of the basement stairs he'd fallen down.

Parker pointed at the other name. "Would that be Rosenstein? Matt Rosenstein?"

"Rosenstein, yes," she said, smiling, pleased with them both. "And the initial is M. So you would know these people."

"Oh, yes, I know them," Parker said. "And the Russian was right. They're going to be very useful to me."

"I think this one," Claire said. She pirouetted, showing off for him and the mirror. Seeing his face in the mirror, she smiled and said, "I think we're both getting what we want."

11

The restaurant was around the corner from Madison Avenue, three blocks from Madame Irina. Inside, it was crowded, tables too close together, people eating elbow to elbow at the long banquette down the right side. In front of the restaurant, on the sidewalk, only two of the tables within the wrought-iron railing were occupied, one of them by Parker and Claire. It was cool out here, traffic noise from the avenue was constant, but they could talk in private.

Parker waited till they'd ordered and the food had arrived. Then he said, "Every once in a while, something that was old that was supposed to be done with, comes back and has to be dealt with again. This is one of those."

"Tell me about it."

"A few years ago," he said, "while I was away on a job, you went to see some people in New Orleans."

"Oh, yes," she said. "Lorraine and Jim."

"I phoned you to wire me money."

"I remember," she said. "You called twice. The first time for five hundred dollars, and the second time for three thousand."

"It was a job that went bad," Parker said. "I came back with nothing."

"You came back," she said.

He shrugged that away. "We were four," he said. "One of them that I didn't know, his name was George Uhl, it turned out he was a crazy. He tried to kill the three of us to keep the money for himself. He got the other two, and I had to go after him. That's when I phoned you."

"George Uhl," she said. "That isn't one of the names you showed Madame Irina."

"No. Uhl is dead now," Parker said. "But he had a friend, this Matt Rosenstein, and Rosenstein dealt himself in to take the money just because he knew it was there. Brock was his partner, or front man. I had to talk with them because they might know where Uhl was. But then they wanted in."

"And those two are still alive," she said.

"When I last saw them," Parker said, "they were both wounded, neither one of them was moving, and they were in a house where they'd been holding a family prisoner. The woman there had no reason to do anything after I left but call the cops. If she called the cops, those two, if they lived, are in jail the rest of their lives. But somehow they're around somewhere, and they sent a fellow to get me. Revenge, I suppose. They have somebody else out there now, watching the house. I'm on another thing, nothing to do with Brock and Rosenstein, and I don't have the time for this distraction now. The other thing'll go down soon, and then I'll see what to do about Brock and Rosenstein."

"But until then," she said, "I can't go to my house."

"I'm sorry for that," he said. "I know you'd rather be there."

"That's all right," she said. "I'll stay in the city until the alterations are done on my coat, and then I'll wear it for a while in Paris."

12

"Good," Elkins said, sounding hurried. "I was hoping you'd call pretty quick."

"I had things to do," Parker said. This pay phone at LaGuardia airport was surrounded by other callers with problems of their own, and the number he'd dialed was a pay phone at a gas station in Great Barrington, Massachusetts, he having ten minutes earlier called Elkins' motel room in the same town to let the phone ring once. Now, hearing the trouble in Elkins' voice, he said, "What went wrong?"

"Larry apparently had a security lapse," Elkins said.

"What, the law got him?"

"No, not that kind. It affects *us*, you and me and Ralph. Come on up here, we'll dope this out."

* * *

The car he chose from long-term parking was a gray Volvo with the parking lot's ticket stuck behind the visor, a date on the ticket of the day before yesterday, and a nearly full gas tank. Three and a half hours later he left it in the municipal parking lot in Great Barrington and walked to the motel, about a mile out north of the main town among the big stores and fast-food restaurants. Elkins was in room 11, and when he opened to Parker's knock Wiss and Lloyd were in there, too. Elkins and Wiss both looked worried, Lloyd mostly embarrassed.

They'd opened the connecting doors between this room and number 12, and brought the chairs from that one in here, so everybody could sit at the round wood-look table under the hanging swag lamp, with Elkins' green Honda and the traffic of state route 7 outside the window. Parker said, "What security? Who found out what?"

"I don't have that part yet," Lloyd told him. "What happened, Mr. Parker, it was just my old habits coming out. I should know better, I'm in a different world now, but I still keep backing everything up."

"Backing what up?" Parker asked him. He would be patient, and he would keep asking questions, and eventually what Lloyd was saying would start to make sense.

"Data," Lloyd said, as though that were an explanation. "I spend most of my time at the computer, you know, though I'm not supposed to, the terms of the parole are I'm supposed to keep away."

"They found you at it?"

"No, no, it's nothing like that." Lloyd shook his head, irritated at himself, then gathered himself for the effort to explain things in a rational way. "It's a hacker," he said. "It's some hacker out there, he came into my file, I'm not sure why, unless one of your names triggered it."

Parker said, "Names? You have a file with our names in it?"

"Yes, that's what I'm saying. I should know better than to keep records, my God, it was my own records brought me down last time, as much as my running around acting out."

Parker said, "What is in this file, besides our names?"

"Well, nothing any more," Lloyd assured him. "As soon as I realized what had happened, I eliminated those files completely, they don't exist, they *never* existed."

"Except they did."

"Yes."

"And somebody read them. What did they find?"

"Names, addresses, phone numbers, places of meetings. Not, thank God," Lloyd said, with a shaky smile, "the subject of the meetings. Nothing about Marino, not *his* name or the hunting lodge or how I plan to cut into his systems or any of that, *that's* all on a secure disk completely separate from the computer. But us, everything about us."

Parker looked at Elkins. "How long has this genius

been flashing my name and address and phone number around?"

Elkins shrugged. "Maybe three days before we first called you. We had things to set up, our old partners to talk to."

So Charov had not been a coincidence. In the old days, Brock had owned a music shop, was a technician, an expert with recording technology. Had he expanded into computers? It seemed a lot of music people had. And all of a sudden he'd found Parker, after all these years, and it had taken three days to get Charov on the case.

Parker looked at Lloyd, who could see he'd somehow made even more trouble than he'd thought. Parker waited, and Lloyd said, "If there's anything I can do . . ."

"This . . . *data* of yours, it's definitely gone?"

"Yes, oh, yes, definitely."

"The guy who came in and got it," Parker said. "Can you follow him home?"

"No, I don't think so," Lloyd said. "Apparently, he got everything he wanted the first time through."

"Yeah, he did," Parker said, and said to the others, "I told you I had this other thing to take care of, and it wasn't connected to you people, but now I think maybe it is connected."

"Because of Larry?" Wiss asked. He seemed very disappointed in his protégé.

"And his files, yeah."

"I'm really sorry," Lloyd said. "Old habits just die hard."

"Some things die easier," Parker told him, and said to the others, "Around the time you called me, a hit man came to visit. A pro out of Russia, with a cover at a liquor importer in New Jersey. I took care of that, but because of being with you people I haven't been able to deal with the people who hired him. I just found out this morning who they are, and I know they got somebody else watching my house right now, waiting for me to come back."

"Stupid, stupid, stupid," Lloyd said to himself.

Wiss said, "We should take a hand. If we brought this guy on you—"

"It's the timing," Elkins said to Wiss. "Sure we brought this guy on him."

"That's what I'm saying," Wiss agreed. "What we got to do is take a hand, make Parker whole again. We want him thinking about *our* little deal, not some guy with a hard-on watching the house."

Again Lloyd said, "If there's anything I—"

"I'm pretty sure there is," Parker told him. "What's at the house right now is a tiny camera, like the size of a wine cork, over the front door frame, with a wire hanging down, so when the door opens it broadcasts the view of the room. That way, they know it's me, or they know it's the cleaning woman, or they know whoever it is and what to do. This is a house on a lake with most of the houses closed for the winter, so the base could be anywhere around there. I thought I didn't have time to deal with it until I was done with you people, but now I think we got to deal with this problem first."

Elkins said, "To get that distraction out of your mind, I agree."

"Not just that," Parker said. "One of the two guys behind this is a fella named Matt Rosenstein that's a heavy heister himself, or used to be. Him and the other guy, Brock, they've got to have some money on them right now, to be throwing it around the way they are, but I know Rosenstein, and he likes to go where money is and take it for himself. That was what our trouble was in the old days. Your boy Lloyd here says he put everything except my blood type in his computer, but *didn't* put anything about Marino's gold toilets or his stashed art gallery, and maybe he didn't. But just to be on the safe side," Parker said, "I'd like to make sure in my own mind, when I go back to that hunting lodge, Matt Rosenstein and Paul Brock aren't gonna be there to say hello."

TWO

1

Lloyd's car was a black Honda Accord, several years old, with a dented right front fender, hair-thin lines of red in the dents to suggest he'd one time run into a fireplug. Parker drove, Lloyd in the front seat beside him, happy to be a passenger. Elkins and Wiss were on their way home, outside Chicago, to wait to learn what Parker and Lloyd had found at Claire's house.

They had to make this trip in the other direction first because Lloyd needed some equipment to bring with him. Part of the equipment was to find the base linked to that camera at the house, and the rest of it was to keep the state of Massachusetts from learning that Lloyd had broken his parole again.

Lloyd lived outside Springfield, about forty-five miles east of Great Barrington. There was a more direct state road, but in the latter part of a weekday afternoon that would be full of shoppers and salarymen, so Parker took them north first to the Mass Pike, then east. The early part of the trip, Lloyd threw out a few more apologies and I'm-stupids, but then Parker said, "That's done. Now we're doing what we're doing now," and after that Lloyd calmed down.

The next time he broke the silence was just after they made the turn onto the Mass Pike, amid the lanes of thundering trucks and rushing imports, when he said, "I'm wondering if Otto ever mentioned you."

"Mainzer? Why would he?"

"There were two things Otto liked to do in prison," Lloyd said. "Fight and talk. He liked to tell stories about his great capers, the ones where he *didn't* get caught. I wondered if you were ever in those stories."

"Did he put names in the stories?"

"Not usually, no."

"He wouldn't," Parker said.

Lloyd studied Parker's profile a minute, digesting that, and then he looked out at the yellow-gray world ahead, backlit by the late-afternoon sun behind them, the black shadows of all these vehicles leaping forward, and what he said was actually a continuation of the conversation, though it didn't sound like it: "I think I'm learning more about this new world since I've been out here than in all the time I was inside."

"You're a quick study," Parker told him. "You'll learn."

"I don't have much choice," Lloyd said. Which was true.

*　　*　　*

"I don't think you should come in," Lloyd told him, as they neared his neighborhood. "You're a bad companion, you know. In fact, you probably shouldn't even stop at the house. Just let me off at the corner and circle a couple times."

"Fine."

Lloyd reached under the dash, between them, and hit some sort of switch. "That's my two-way to the house," he said. "When I'm ready to come out, I'll tell you."

"Good."

"If you need to speak to me about anything," Lloyd went on, "you see the white button over by the side vent?"

The hole for the button had been drilled neatly, but it was still clearly a non-factory add-on. "Yeah," Parker said.

"Push that and just speak. I'll hear you."

"Who've you got at home?"

"No one any more." Lloyd seemed embarrassed. "My wife decided on a divorce two years after I went in."

"That happens."

"The counselor said so, yes. Also, I have cousins that visit sometimes, so we use the radio."

"Uh-huh."

"You'll let me off two blocks from here."

This part of West Springfield, just west of the Connecticut River, was a neat working-class grid of older two-story one-family homes, most with porches and cropped lawns, many with children's toys scattered around the front. Traffic was light, and very local. A stranger wouldn't get to stay here long without being noticed.

Parker said, "How long do you think? Before you come out."

"Oh, ten minutes, no more."

"I'll drive out of the neighborhood and then back."

"All right, fine. Up ahead here, by that brick church."

Parker pulled to the curb, looking around. "And where are you from here?"

Lloyd pointed away to the right. "Half a block, number three-eighty-seven. But don't come to the house!"

"No, I'll wait back here."

"Okay, good."

Lloyd got out and walked away, a bedraggled but earnest figure, a guy who'd had a wife and a house in this modest neighborhood, when he was supposed to be rich instead, and had gone nuts when he'd found out, and was still trying to become some new guy, not yet sure who that new guy was. His openness and malleability had clearly helped him survive inside, but would do less for him out here. He was what Wiss and Elkins needed on the technical side, but Parker wondered how much of a liability he was going to be on the personal side.

He drove the Honda away from there, straight for half a dozen blocks, then a left for a few blocks, then another left, and then faintly heard crackling noises, static inside the car. Lloyd's radio? Had he turned it on in the house?

Yes. And was speaking: "... nobody gets hurt ... how can it get back to *you*? It can't." And wasn't Lloyd.

"If I knew where he was, I'd tell you." *That* was Lloyd. "I'm not a brave man, look at me, I'm scared to death of you two. If I knew, I'd tell."

So Brock and Rosenstein's second team had decided Parker wasn't going back to the house on the lake, not right away, so they might as well try to get at him through one of the other names they'd picked up from Lloyd's computer. And they'd gone straight to the weakest link.

"I tell you what," said a third voice, as Parker made the left and saw the brick church some distance ahead. "You tell us another story first, just to get into the mood for it."

"Story? What story?"

"The job you're pulling with the other three. Tell us about that."

"Oh, I can't do that!"

"Sure you can."

Parker pulled to the curb a block short of the church, by a branch library. His pistol was in his inside jacket pocket. The electric garage door opener from the visor he put into the right outer pocket, then got out of the Honda, left it unlocked, and went for a walk.

* * *

There wouldn't be time to come at this with indirection. Lloyd wouldn't stand up to those people for a second, and once they'd squeezed him, why not kill him? Even if they didn't do that, once he'd failed he'd have one more defeat to brood about when he should be thinking about Paxton Marino's security instead.

There is a thing called loser mentality, and losing is both its cause and symptom. It's clearly what had sent Lloyd on his rampage once before, and if he got another bout of the same illness he'd be no good to Parker and the others. Which was bad because, the way it looked, there was no job without Larry Lloyd.

The house was dark shingle, up ahead on the left, set back from the sidewalk behind a neat lawn, like all the other houses along here. Its wide front porch had a green shingle roof held up by square stone pillars, inside which the house looked muffled, almost abandoned. On its left side, nearest Parker as he approached, a one-car attached garage had been added at a later date, done in the same style but somehow not the same at all. The blacktop driveway to the garage was obscured on this side by a low privet hedge, put in by the neighbor. On a block where most of the houses were clapboard, in white or pastels, Lloyd's house *looked* like the one with secrets.

Parker didn't pause. Rounding the hedge, he strode up the driveway, trusting that the two inside would concentrate on Lloyd and not look out the windows. As he neared the brown-painted wooden overhead door, he pulled the opener from his pocket and thumbed the button. The door jerked, started its slide upward, and he went down to the blacktop, landing on his left side. He rolled through the gap under the door, thumbing the opener again—the door stopped—and again—it started down—then rolled across the empty concrete floor to the right wall, near the house, dropping the opener and reaching inside the jacket for his gun.

Would the few seconds of the opener motor have been heard inside the house? Would it have been recognized, in that short a time? Parker got to his knees then, holding the pistol in both hands aimed at the connecting door to the house. In that posture, he slid his right shoulder up the wall until he was on his feet.

No sound, no apparent movement. There was no time to be sure of anything; he slipped along the wall, listened for two seconds at the door, turned the knob with his left hand, pushed.

Sounds, some distance away. Blubbering. Broken already.

Parker went through a messy kitchen, without really seeing it, concentrating on the doorway beyond, the sounds from beyond that. Into a dark hall, a dining room through a doorway opposite, some muddied daylight from the lace-curtained glass in the front door down to the right. Sobbing from down that way.

The hall carpet silenced his feet. He came swiftly down the hall, pistol ahead of himself, spun into the living room doorway, and put a bullet into the knee of the one on the left.

The tableau froze for one second, paralyzed by the sound of the shot. Making the turn, he'd seen Lloyd's back to him as he slumped on his knees at the coffee table fronting the sofa on the far wall, shoulders heaving as he wept, arm moving as he wrote on a sheet of paper on the coffee table. The two strangers hulked on either side of him and back a pace, both standard-issue thugs, big but ordinary. He needed one of them alive at the end of this, to answer questions. The one on the right held a sap, long and flexible, that would hurt wherever it hit, but the one on the left held the 9mm Beretta, so it was the one on the left Parker brought down first.

The other was a surprise. He heard the shot, he saw the tableau dissolve as his partner began to crumble and Lloyd's head jerked upward, and without ever looking in Parker's direction he wheeled on his right foot, folded his forearms over the top of his head, and launched himself through the living room's picture window.

"Get the gun and *keep* that one!" Parker yelled at Lloyd, turned, and ran out the front door.

The other one was just vaulting the porch rail. Parker snapped a shot at him, but knew it was no good, and knew he couldn't do any more shooting, not here, not now. The other guy, face and forearms bleeding, ran across the lawn, and Parker saw a passing driver give the scene a curious look.

He wanted them both, he needed them both, but he couldn't chase a bleeding man in a family neighborhood in the middle of the afternoon. And how long could he trust Lloyd to keep the first one, even with a bullet in him? Reluctant, but knowing there was no choice, Parker went back into the house.

Lloyd was alone in the living room, curled up in a fetal position on the floor, face into the carpet. He heard Parker come in, and lifted a tear-stained face that was astonishingly smiling; but then he uncurled enough to show he still had the Beretta, clutched in both hands. That was the reason for the smile; he hadn't let a knee-shot man take the pistol away from him.

Parker spread his hands, asking the question, and Lloyd nodded jerkily at the connecting doorway to the dining room. Parker started toward that doorway, then realized that was the mistake. The guy's knee was gone; how fast could he move, and for how long?

Parker went out to the hall and down to the dining room that way. When he eased his head around the frame, he saw the guy just to the right of the other door, Lloyd still visible through there on the floor, the guy leaning heavily against the wall, blood soaking his right pants leg from the knee down, his hands clenched on a chair he'd dragged over from the dining room table. He wanted Parker to come through that doorway and take the chair in the face.

No. Parker stepped into the dining room, showed the pistol, and said, "Sit on it. You'll feel better."

The guy looked at him. He was in pain, but he was

still trying to find a way out of here. His eyes flicked at the side windows.

Parker said, "I don't think so. You want him to come back, and so do I, but I don't think so. Sit down, it's still question time."

The guy thought about that, then shook his head. "I'm just the heavy lifter," he said, wheezing as he talked. "My partner knows everything."

"You know some—"

Lloyd came erupting out of the other room, face twisted, grimacing with hatred and shame and revenge. "You *bastard*!" he yelled, and stuck the Beretta into the middle of the guy's face, and pulled the trigger.

2

Parker stepped forward, knocked the Beretta away, knocked Lloyd to the ground, but it was too late. The thug's head was splattered on the wall now, and his body had dropped like a sack of doorknobs.

Lloyd, on his side on the floor, stared in horror at the man he'd just killed. "My God," he whispered.

"I needed him," Parker said. "*You* needed him. And you don't need this mess."

"I didn't— I don't know what I—"

"You got tough all of a sudden," Parker told him. "Get up. Stop looking at him, get up, come into the other room, we'll work this out."

Lloyd finally looked away from the dead man, blinking up at Parker. "I was just . . . scared," he said.

"Come in here," Parker said again, and went back to the living room, where the furniture was a little messed up, not too bad, and the broken window didn't show very much under the dark porch roof. He stood looking at the room, considering it, until Lloyd came in, shaky, unsure of his balance. Then Parker sat on the sofa, put his feet on the coffee table, on the story Lloyd had been writing, and said, "You want to give this place up? Or you want to deal with what happened? Sit down."

"Do I want to— What do you mean, give this place up?"

"Sit *down*."

Lloyd sat, on the chair angled to Parker's right. He stayed forward on the seat, knees together, hands clasped on knees, worried face turned to Parker. He said, "Move? How can I move?"

"You've got two choices," Parker told him. "You can give up being on parole, hide out, take your profit from the Montana job and turn yourself into somebody else. Or you can clean up this mess."

"I can't— I can't—"

"You *can* do either one. They're both gonna be tough."

Lloyd looked at the doorway. "That man—"

Parker said, "How much does the law watch this house?"

"What? Oh, the patrol." Lloyd shook his head, to clear it. "City police keep an eye on me," he said. "In a car, the regular patrol car. Not often. They just drive by, I see them look at the place, they drive by."

"They never come in?"

"Once or twice, if something's different. A strange

car in the driveway, other people here." He made a twisted smile. "They want to be sure everybody knows I'm a felon."

"What about when you drive away from here? Stop you, search the car?"

"A few times they stopped me," Lloyd said, shrugging that away. "Just ask me where I'm going, remind me I'm on a leash."

"Search the car?"

"Never."

"Do you have a tarp?"

Lloyd didn't seem to know the word. "A what?"

"A large waterproof sheet," Parker told him. "Plastic, whatever."

"Oh, yes, sure. In the basement. You mean for"—a glance at the doorway—"him."

"You wrap him good," Parker said. "Then you clean up in there. You got any caulk, for windows, anything like that?"

"Yes, probably."

"The bullet's in the wall," Parker said. "After you clean the wall, plug the hole with anything you got that'll dry hard. It's a small hole, don't worry about color. And it didn't come through on this side."

Lloyd hadn't noticed that. Now he gave this wall a surprised look and said, "All right."

"When everything's clean, and it's rolled in the tarp," Parker said, "call a glazier, say you were moving"—he looked around the room—"that bookcase, and it tipped and broke the window."

"Shouldn't I say somebody threw a stone at the house? There *is* harassment here, sometimes. People around here know the story."

"The glass is on the porch," Parker reminded him, "not in here. Say it's a rush job, you need it today. Then . . ." Parker took the Honda keys out of his pocket and tossed them to Lloyd, who caught them two-handed. "Then you go get your car. It's beyond the church, by the library. The opener's on the floor in the garage."

"All right," Lloyd said.

"Put the package in the trunk," Parker said, "and the other stuff you need in the car. Then wait for the glazier."

"You mean he has to come today."

"Sure he has to come today, it's an emergency, you can't leave a living room window broken overnight. Once he comes and fixes it and goes, you take a drive, get rid of the package where nobody sees you and it can't come back to screw you up later."

"There's the river, I could do that."

"Whatever you want. Then come back and get me and we'll get out of here."

"This is gonna take hours," Lloyd said. "What will you be doing?"

"Sleep," Parker said, and stood. "You got a spare room?"

Standing, doubtful, Lloyd said, "There's a cot in my office. Upstairs."

"Good," Parker said.

*   *   *

It wasn't real sleep, but something close, learned a long time ago, a way to rest the body and the brain, a kind of trance, awareness of the outer world sheathed in unawareness. The dim room remained, shades drawn over both windows, the gray-canvas-covered synthesizer in which Lloyd kept his computer equipment not so much concealed as reconfigured, the shelves and cabinets, the closed door, the framed color photographs of machines, the small occasional sounds from outside the room, and the cot, narrow, with a thin mattress covered by a Canadian wool blanket in broad bands of gray and green and black that held him like a cupped hand. Inside it, farther within it, there was nothing except the small bubbles of awareness that surfaced and surfaced and found nothing wrong.

Parker had told Lloyd, "Knock," because, before lying on the cot, he'd leaned the gangly metal synthesizer chair off-kilter sideways against the knob. When the knock sounded and Lloyd's distant small voice called, "Parker," he woke at once and sat up, and the gray rectangles of the shaded windows were now black.

"All right," he answered. "I'll be down in a few minutes." And switched on the light, took the pistol from under the pillow, put on his shoes, moved the chair back from the door.

When he came downstairs, face washed, rested, still stretching the sleep out of his shoulders, Lloyd was seated on the sofa in the living room. He stood when Parker entered. "All set," he said.

Parker looked at the empty nighttime street through the new window glass. Lights in houses across the way seemed a canyon distant. He said, "Everything cleaned up?"

"Oh, yes," Lloyd said, with grim emphasis.

Parker looked at him. Lloyd was pale, but under control. "You're okay now," he said.

"I think so." Lloyd grinned and shook his head. "When I went to jail," he said, "I told myself, now I've really learned not to lose control, the bad things that can happen if I lose control. I'll never lose control again, I said, I've learned my lesson."

"Uh-huh."

Lloyd looked over at the dining room doorway, then back at Parker. "I was wrong," he said. "But this time, if I haven't learned anything, there's no hope for me."

"You did okay," Parker said. "Except when you got excited."

"That's the part I'm talking about," Lloyd said. "The tarp was slippery, you know. Heavy, and slippery, and hard to get a grip on. I thought the washing, the wall, that was going to be the worst, but it was the slippery tarp."

Driving west on the Mass Pike, not yet midnight, Parker at the wheel, Lloyd said, "I want to thank you."

"Don't have to."

"After I screwed up, after I . . . shot that fellow, you had every right to take it out on me, or just walk away. We *did* need him, talk to him, I know we did. But you stayed, you put me back together again, and I want to thank you for it."

Parker shrugged, watching the trucks ahead. "We need you for the job," he said.

3

Mrs. Elkins?"

"Yes?" Wary, never knowing, when Frank was away, whether a phone call was good or bad.

"It's Parker." He'd never met the woman, but he'd left messages with her before.

"Yes?" Still wary; it could still be good or bad.

"Frank's on his way home," Parker told her.

"Good."

"Would you tell him my friends might drop in."

"Friends of yours?"

"He'll know," Parker said, and hung up, and went back to the Honda, where Lloyd was a pale disembodied face in the distant gas station lights. This was the same station where he'd talked with Elkins first, after getting rid of Charov, just a few miles from Claire's house, and it was three in the morning, the station closed.

Getting behind the wheel, he said, "We'll park at the lake, by one of the empty houses."

"A strange place to live," Lloyd said. "Where all the houses are empty."

There was nothing to say to that. Parker drove away from the gas station and up to the turn where the sign pointed to Colliver's Pond. He drove halfway from the turn toward Claire's house, then chose a driveway on the right leading up to one of the less desirable, less expensive houses without lake frontage.

Blank tan rectangles of plywood covering the windows stared down on them before Parker switched off the headlights. Most of the householders around here merely locked their places and went away at the end of each summer, but a few acted as though winter was the return of the Ice Age.

Parker and Lloyd walked along the road that circled the lake. There were no streetlights out here, so when the houses were empty the nights were very dark. A smallish moon low in the sky over their left shoulders helped them pick out the pavement of the roadway, and showed Parker the mailbox marked WILLIS. Keeping his voice low, he said, "It's in there. I'll wait. Just don't go in the house."

"I don't have to. What electricity do you have on?"

"None. We shut it off at the box."

"Phone on?"

"Yes."

"Do you know where the service comes in?"

"Left corner, over the garage."

In his element now, playing with his machines, Lloyd was calm and confident. Taking a small device like a photographer's light meter from his pocket, he pressed the button on its side that made the dim light shine on the dial. Shielding that with one hand, he looked at the dial, turned the meter left and right, and said, "Something. Faint. Could be coming from in there. I won't be long."

Lloyd faded into the darkness of the driveway, under the trees, and Parker stood near the mailbox, watching the empty road. He remembered how smoothly and briskly Lloyd had done his work at Paxton Marino's lodge. If they could keep this other stress away from him, he'd be fine, but when he got emotional he was like a dog that needed to be shot.

Lloyd was back in less than ten minutes. "I guess there's something in there," he said, "but not sending, receiving. There's a signal coming in from down that way." Farther along the road.

"That's the base," Parker said. "Anybody opens that door, the camera will start to send. Can you find the base?"

"I should be able to," Lloyd said. "When we get nearer, the signal's going to be stronger. If we pass it, the signal will change, then get weaker."

"Good," Parker said.

Lloyd now carried a mini earphone, like ones used with cellphones, attached to that dial. Fixing it to his right ear, he started walking, slowly, listening to electricity in the night, while Parker walked beside him, watching, looking at the darkness, then seeing light ahead, amber light from the windows of a house on the lake.

Lloyd had seen it, too. "Not every house is empty," he said.

"There are some year-rounders," Parker agreed. "They're asleep now."

"This could be insomnia," Lloyd suggested. "But the signal is getting stronger."

Either the road was closer to the lake here or the house was set back farther from the shore, because it was more visible than Claire's house, nearer, through fewer trees. What looked like living room windows gleamed through the tree trunks on the left front of the low house, with darkness on the right. The driveway was farther left.

Lloyd said, "Should we go in?"

"No. Walk by, see if the signal changes."

"It's changing right now," Lloyd said. "This is where it's coming from."

The time for machinery was finished. "Wait here," Parker said. He backtracked to the next driveway, for the next house over, dark and silent. He walked down the driveway, then through the scrub and trees to the house with the lights.

This place didn't have a garage. The gravel driveway ended beside the house, with an older Volvo station wagon parked there. A side door with small windows in it led into a kitchen that he could see in lightspill from the doorway beyond.

He moved cautiously around the front of the house until he reached the first lit widow. Edging forward, he saw a doorway to the front hall, then a side wall with a low sofa surmounted by comical prints of fishermen, then the far wall, all windows for the view of the lake, and then, close to this window, a floor lamp with a yellow shade and, next to it, a man in a red tartan chair with wooden arms, reading a book.

Parker looked in at him in one-quarter profile, seeing a wrinkled but bony face and neck, silver-framed eyeglasses, a nearly bald head with some remaining thin white hair, a prominent pale ear, hard jawline, red-and-black flannel shirt. The hands holding the hardcover book were gnarled and big-knuckled.

There was no one else in the room. There was no indication of anybody else around. Parker moved away from the light, listened to the night, heard nothing he didn't expect. He walked past the lit windows to the front door, knocked on it, and took the pistol from his pocket.

When the man opened the door, Parker saw he had to be in his seventies at least, tall but stooped, thinner than he used to be. He looked at Parker with only mild curiosity, surprised that anyone could come around at such an hour, then saw the pistol, just there, not pointed at him or anywhere in particular, and he gave a startled jerk, moving back a pace, saying, "Good God!" Then he blinked at Parker, realized he was being neither shot nor directly threatened, and said, "Well— I suppose you're coming in."

Parker, staying outside the doorway, said, "Who else is here?"

"My wife," the man said, nodding toward the other end of the house. "She's asleep."

Parker turned and called, not loud, "Lloyd." Then he stepped into the house, saying to the man, "Leave it open."

"Whatever you say."

Parker stepped into the living room, saw no weapons anywhere, saw the book now closed with a marker in it on the chair the man had been sitting in, and saw the television set on the other side of the room, next to the kitchen doorway, facing the sofa. There were two boxes on top of it, one for cable and one for something else. The set would be visible from where the man sat in the chair.

Lloyd came in, looking curiously at the older man. "What's happening?"

"Close the door," Parker said. "He says he has a wife asleep here and nobody else. Get her up."

"I wish you wouldn't," the man said. He was reasonable, neither afraid nor belligerent.

Parker looked at him, waiting.

The man said, "She has diabetes, among other things. She needs a regular pattern in her life."

"So she watches by day and you watch by night, is that it?"

The man smiled, as though at himself, and shook his head. "Of course that's who you are," he said. "Yes, that's what we do. But you can leave her out of it."

"I don't think so." Parker turned to Lloyd, pointing at the extra box on top of the television set. "Is that it?"

"It should be," Lloyd said. He went over to look at the box without touching it. "Yes, this is it."

Parker turned back to the man. "You want to get your wife yourself? Lloyd will go with you."

"It really isn't necessary," the man said. "I'll tell you what I know, and she knows less than I do. I'm prepared to cooperate, but I'd like you to bend just a little here. My wife's a sound sleeper, she'll never know you were even in the house."

Parker considered. Having him calm and talking was better, if possible. He said, "Is there a phone in the bedroom?"

"Yes."

To Lloyd, Parker said, "Go get it. If she wakes up, bring her along. If not, leave her there."

"Thank you," the man said, and to Lloyd, "It's the second door on the left."

Lloyd went through the hallway, and Parker said, "Any other phones in the house, besides that one?" Pointing at the phone on the round table to the left of where the man had been reading.

"In the kitchen, that's all."

Lloyd came back with a phone in his hand. "Snoring," he said, and put the phone down.

The man said, "That embarrasses her, but she can't stop. It's made it easier for me to be a night owl."

Parker said to Lloyd, "Did you look around?"

"No other people," Lloyd said, "and no other phones."

"Good." To the man, Parker said, "You're waiting for something to show on the television."

"That's right."

"What?"

"A living room," the man said. "It's in a house about a quarter mile down that way."

"What are you supposed to do when it comes on?"

"That depends," the man said. "If it's the cleaning lady, which it has been once, then I merely push the off button on the box and it shuts itself off. If it's you, on the other hand—"

Parker said, "They showed you a picture of me?"

"No, a verbal description," the man said, "but accurate. A big man, hard but shaggy, with brown flat hair. They particularly mentioned the long arms and large hands, with prominent veins."

"All right. What are you supposed to do if it's me?"

"There's a phone number I'm to call, let it ring twice, hang up. Then Marie and I are to pack and go home and they'll send us a check for the rest of the money."

"Where's this phone number?"

The man pointed at the table next to where he'd been reading. "Over there, under the phone."

Parker went over, moved the phone, found a small square of white paper beneath it from a Marriott Hotel memo pad. A seven-digit number was on the paper, nothing else. He said, "What area code?"

"None," the man said. "It's a local call."

Parker frowned. He didn't like that. Moving away from the table, leaving the paper out next to the phone, he said, "Sit down again, where you were."

"All right." He went over to pick up his book, then sit. With a small rueful smile, he said, "I don't believe I'll read," and put the book on the floor on the other side from the phone table.

Parker stood in the middle of the room, looking around, thinking. Lloyd watched him, then said, "What's wrong?"

"Don't know yet."

It should be the shooter here, not a watchdog. They're waiting for Parker to come home, walk into his house. The minute the camera sees him, the shooter should be on his way. But they do this thing instead, hire some couple to make a homey look, an extra phone call to a shooter somewhere nearby, but why? Why isn't the shooter the one looking at the television set?

Parker pointed to the sofa, and told Lloyd, "Sit there. Listen for the wife. Or anything else."

"You don't like this setup, do you?" Lloyd asked.

Parker crossed to the kitchen, took a wooden chair from there, brought it back to the living room, placed it where he could sit in front of the man but off-center, so Lloyd could still see them both. He said, "Tell me your name."

"Hembridge. Arthur."

"Arthur or Art?"

Another rueful smile. "I used to be Art. I seem to be Arthur these days."

"You took a strange job here, Arthur," Parker said.

"I don't get much of anything to do any more," Arthur said. "It's good to have a little extra in your kick."

"How come it's *your* job? Who hired you?"

"Fella I used to know in my working days," Arthur said.

"Where did you work, Arthur?"

Arthur leaned back, thoughtful, looking from Parker to Lloyd and back to Parker. "I don't believe I know you two," he said.

Parker said, "You worked on the wrong side of the law."

"Maybe we could leave it at that," Arthur said.

"This fella— You still in touch with him?"

"Hadn't heard from him in eight years."

"Gives you a call, offers you a job, money's good enough but not great, you aren't doing anything else, the wife says it might make a nice change, you say okay."

"That's about it."

"This fella isn't a close friend," Parker suggested.

Arthur shrugged. "We always got along. Never close, you know."

"I know." Parker leaned forward, elbows on knees, watching Arthur's face. "When you left to come out here," he said, "this fella gave you something you were supposed to leave behind, for the people who'd take over after you made the phone call."

Arthur frowned at him. "I don't know where you're heading here," he said.

Parker leaned back. "Did they tell you what the surveillance was for?"

"A fella used to be with them," Arthur said, "they think flipped for Customs, then he disappeared. They want to know what he gave them, what they have to change."

"Talk to him. That what you believe?"

Arthur shook his head. "I don't know what's likely to happen after the conversation," he said. "That's not my department. But I believe it starts with talk, yes, so they know what their exposure is. Maybe it all turns out to be a misunderstanding, no problem after all." Arthur spread his hands, beginning to look baffled. "It's *you* we're talking about, after all," he said. "Don't *you* know what's going on?"

"I'm beginning to," Parker said. "I never worked for or with these friends of yours, Arthur. I don't have anything to do with Customs. These people have a contract out on me, a straight hit. So somewhere around here there's a shooter, waiting for your call. Right?"

"If it's just a contract," Arthur said, "then, sure, I suppose there is."

"*You* were never a hit man."

"Good God, no!"

"I didn't think so," Parker said. "So the shooter's

somebody else. But why isn't *he* in this room, watching that TV?"

"Well, you would have found him, wouldn't you," Arthur said, "about five minutes ago."

"Arthur," Parker said, "he isn't here because you *are* it. When you dial that number, there's a house about a quarter mile from here that blows up."

Lloyd said, "Of course! *That's* the way to do it."

"How would you feel, Arthur," Parker asked him, "if you were watching the TV and dialing the number and that house blew up, close enough to wake your wife?"

"That wasn't the deal," Arthur said. He looked offended. "Right in the neighborhood? The cops could be on *me*, first thing you know."

"You know them," Parker said, "but you're not tight with them. They don't have to waste some useful guy's time here, they can just leave you and your wife in this house they rented in your name, and if I never do come home then after a while they pay you off and that's the end of it. But if I *do* come home, and you see me, and you dial that number, and you see and hear the house go up, why would they want to keep you around?"

Arthur watched him, eyes wide and jaw clenched.

Parker said, "Let's have a look at that package, Arthur, the one you were supposed to not open, just leave behind here after you go away."

4

always mistrusted that rotten bastard," Arthur said.

Lloyd said, "Parker, do you think so? Two bombs?"

"You'll tell me," Parker said, "as soon as Arthur gives you the package."

They both looked at Arthur, who started to get up, stopped himself, almost said two or three things, then sat back and said, "Give me a second here."

Parker watched him. "For what?"

"I never did like it when things got sudden," Arthur told him, "and I like it even less now. People talk fast, you go along, sure you say, sure, and all of a sudden you're someplace you don't want to be."

Parker sat back in the chair, crossing one leg over the other. "Take your time," he said.

"We trotted through this pretty good," Arthur explained, "but now I got to back up and remind myself, nobody needs to kill *me*."

"Nobody needs to keep you alive, either," Parker told him. "What use are you?"

"Some little use," Arthur said. "I sit here and wait for you to come home. Then I dial that number there. Why isn't that to somebody else near here, ready to move in on you? This way, you can get to me, but you can't get to him."

"Through that number, I can."

Arthur looked at the numbers written on the sheet from the memo pad. "That's true."

"And now they'd have to go set up another whole household, twenty-four hours a day, ready to go when you ring their phone. How many shooters? They'd need somebody awake, whenever the call came."

"That's also true," Arthur said.

"It's simpler to blow me up," Parker told him. "But then they still have you here, a witness, too close to the scene, you'll never get away before the law arrives, your name is probably all over this rental."

"It is," Arthur agreed.

"Why would they want to leave you around," Parker asked him, "to decide for yourself if you'd rather answer questions or spend the rest of your life in the can?"

Arthur slowly nodded, then turned toward Lloyd. "It's in the kitchen," he said. "Under the sink."

Lloyd stood. "I'll get it."

"Just a box wrapped in brown paper," Arthur told him. "Cigar box size."

Lloyd went into the kitchen, and Arthur looked at Parker. "The fella's name," he said, "is Frank Meany."

"That recruited you."

"That's right."

Lloyd came back with the box, holding it flat in both hands. "Give me a minute with this," he said. He went back to the sofa, put the box on the coffee table, sat down, and spent a while merely looking it over, not touching it.

Arthur said, "I worked forty years for those people. Driver, then boss. I organized and ran two routes north, one through New York, one through Maine to Halifax."

"You said Customs before," Parker said. "So you were smuggling."

"Cigarettes north, out of DC, where you don't have the state and local taxes," Arthur said. "Whiskey south. It isn't a crime against people, it's a crime against the tax man, the closest thing you got to a victimless crime. No violence, or at least usually. Good profit. I don't see where killing has to come into it at this late date."

Lloyd had taken a penknife from his pocket, and carefully sliced away the brown paper and brown packaging tape. Inside it actually was a cigar box, with pictures of flamenco dancers on the lid and sides. Lloyd lifted the box away from the brown paper, put it down by itself, brushed the brown paper to the floor, and leaned close to study the box.

Parker said, "I'm trying to remember a name. An outfit in Bayonne."

Arthur gave him a sharp look. "What kind of outfit?"

"Cosmopolitan, that was it," Parker said. "Cosmopolitan Beverages."

"Wait a minute," Arthur said, beginning to have doubts again. "If you're nothing to do with Customs, nothing to do with Cosmopolitan, how do you *know* about it?"

"The first hitter they sent," Parker told him, "was a Russian with a cover at Cosmopolitan. The people in the office there never heard of him, but he had papers on him showed he worked for them, had his green card, could travel anywhere he wanted."

"Here goes nothing," Lloyd said, and lifted the lid.

The other two looked at him. Absorbed, he gazed into the box. "Cigars," he said.

Parker stood and crossed over to look into the box. Slender long cigars, dark brown leaf, lay in a neat tight row, packed edge to edge in the box, flattened slightly along their upper surfaces from the pressure of the lid.

Arthur had stayed where he was, but was curious. "It's *cigars*?"

"On top," Lloyd said, and pointed to the end of the last cigar on the right. "See that wire?"

Parker had to lean close to see it; another hair-thin wire, like the one to trigger the camera at Claire's house, except this one was coiled around the end of the cigar.

Arthur had come over. "What is it?"

"A little wire," Lloyd said, and pointed at it.

Arthur took off his glasses with both hands, folded the wings, and bent close to look where Lloyd was pointing. "Son of a bitch," he said, and straightened, and put his glasses back on.

Lloyd said, "This is as deep into this box as I want to go."

"We don't have to go any more," Parker said. "We all know what the story is now. Don't we, Arthur?"

Arthur sighed. "I would have called that number," he said.

They all looked at the row of cigars in the open box. Then Lloyd lifted his head. "I haven't heard snoring for a while," he said.

Arthur said, "Well, she doesn't snore *all* the time."

"Look," Parker said.

Lloyd nodded and got to his feet and left the room.

"She's a heavy sleeper," Arthur insisted.

They waited, and Lloyd came back. "She's gone."

"Damn!" Arthur cried. "She must of woke herself up, she wakes herself up sometimes with the snoring, rolls over, goes back to sleep."

"Heard voices," Lloyd suggested.

"Probably looked in here from the hall," Arthur said. "Recognized you from the description."

"There's a bedroom window open," Lloyd said. "Wasn't open before."

"She's got to be in robe and slippers," Arthur said.

He looked anxious, bewildered. "Where's she gonna *go?*"

Parker turned to answer him, and saw the television on. "There," he said, pointing.

They all looked. The set had switched on, to show them an interior too dark to clearly make out. There seemed to be movement there.

Arthur said, "She went to your place? What's she *doing* there?"

Parker said, "Looking for the phone."

5

Picking up Arthur's phone, punching out Claire's number, Parker said, "Does your wife know this number on the paper?"

"She should," he said. "The both of us have been looking at it for days, that's why I put it under the phone. You calling your place?"

In Parker's ear, the ringing began.

Lloyd said, "You're showing her where the phone is."

"She'll find it anyway," Parker said. The ringing kept on. Turning, he extended the receiver to Arthur, saying, "When she picks up, talk to her."

"I will." Arthur listened to the earpiece.

Lloyd said, "What if she picks it up just for a second, then breaks the connection so she can make her own call?"

"Arthur talks fast," Parker said.

Parker and Lloyd watched Arthur, whose forehead now showed a whole new array of creases. They waited, and Lloyd said, "Maybe I should—" and Arthur yelled, *"Joyce!"*

He blinked. He looked at Parker. "She hung up."

Parker turned to push the cutoff, then redial, then turned back. Arthur listened, and listened, and sagged. Lowering the phone, he said, "Busy."

Parker took a step backward, away from the phone. Lloyd looked at Parker as though he thought some instructions would be coming now. Arthur put the receiver back in its cradle, then looked at it. "What did I hang it up for?" he asked.

They waited, listening to nothing. Arthur took his glasses off, folded the wings, put the glasses in his shirt pocket. He rubbed his eyes with thumb and first finger of his right hand. He looked tired.

"I saw this movie," Lloyd said. "I didn't like it much."

Nobody answered.

When the phone rang, all three jumped. Arthur grabbed for it, yelled into it, *"Joyce!"*

"I started to dial that other number," Joyce Hembridge explained, sitting on the sofa in her bathrobe and slippers. "I got about halfway through it, but then I realized it was Arthur's voice I'd just heard, so I should talk to him first. I could always make that other the second call."

After Arthur had talked to her on the phone, Lloyd

had taken the Volvo to go bring her back, while Parker talked with Arthur, saying, "Tell me about this Frank Meany."

"He came there a few years before I retired," Arthur said.

"To Cosmopolitan?"

"He was supposed to be a salesman." Arthur shrugged. "Cosmopolitan has a lot of under-the-counter stuff. Like me with the cigarettes and whiskey. Other fellas in the company didn't know what I was doing, and I didn't know what they were doing, and that was fine with everybody."

"But you got to know Meany."

"There was always somebody I was supposed to call," Arthur explained, "if there was any trouble on the routes. A bent cop coming unbent, a driver dipping in for himself, any of the little things that can happen. I'd call the guy and he'd take care of it. The last few years I was there, the guy was Meany. We took a couple trips together, Plattsburgh once, Bangor once, we got along. I knew he was muscle, but that was the job, and he was pleasant with me, liked to talk sports, and he never made me know anything I didn't want to know."

"Where does he live?"

"That I don't know," Arthur said. He glanced over at the phone. "At this point, I wish I did."

"You've got a way to get in touch with him, though," Parker suggested. "Other than that phone number."

"But I don't," Arthur said. "The way it worked, he called me, we met at a diner on route forty-six, he told me about this place, the setup, the story he was telling. He gave me the real estate agent's card and the cigar box and some cash, and I went and signed the lease, and it was as easy as that." Arthur looked surprised, then smiled. "They were setting *me* up, weren't they? From the get-go. No name on the lease but mine. And I never had a bit of trouble with anybody on the job."

"They didn't need you."

Arthur nodded. "I think I need them," he said. "You have it in mind to go talk with Frank?"

"Yes."

"I'd like to talk to him, too," Arthur said, and Lloyd returned then with Joyce, a rangy woman not many years younger than her husband, with a depleted paleness in the flesh of her face that she would normally hide with makeup. She'd thrown a bandana over her head before going out the window here, but steel-gray swatches of wiry hair stuck out from underneath.

When Arthur told her what was going on, she looked around at them, a faint flush on her face, and said, "They were going to kill us. Just like that."

"Explosions are very good," Lloyd told her, "for getting rid of evidence. And you two were going to be evidence, I'm afraid."

She said, "Arthur? What are you going to do about it?"

"Mr. Parker and I were talking about that," Arthur said, and turned to Parker. "I don't know how to find Meany myself, but I've been thinking about it and there's another guy I can reach who'll know where he is."

"Who?"

"Fella named Rafe Hargetty. He took my place when I left there, I broke him in. We talked on the phone sometimes, the first few years. I could still find him."

"Where?" Parker said.

Arthur shook his head. "He'll talk to me, he won't talk to you."

Parker thought it over. Arthur had his own dreams of revenge, which would have to be controlled, but it was true Hargetty was likelier to talk to Arthur than some hard stranger. "Come along, then," he said, and turned to Lloyd. "I can't have a bomb stashed in that other house," he said.

"Not a good time," Lloyd agreed, "for a wrong number."

"Arthur and I will see this Hargetty," Parker said, "and then I'll go on and clean up this business. You stay here, get rid of that cigar box, find the one at the other house and get rid of it."

Lloyd nodded. "Can do."

"When I get back," Parker said, "maybe we can get to Montana at last."

6

That's it there," Arthur said. "I'll just find a place to park."

Parker looked at the building as they drove by it in Arthur's Volvo. A squat two-story brick commercial structure on Hudson Street, just a few blocks north of the Holland Tunnel, most of its downstairs facade was taken up by two wide metal garage doors, painted a dull rust color, with a row of squarish large windows upstairs. To the right of the garage doors was a gray metal door with company names painted on it in gold, and to the right of the building itself was a pale concrete parking area, as broad as the building, half full of delivery vans, sealed at the back and the other side by the dark gray walls of much taller old factory buildings, and fronted on the street side by a chain-link gate in a chain-link fence topped by razor wire.

Arthur drove slowly, looking for a clear space at the

curb, and Parker said, "None of that says Cosmopolitan." The names on the door had been All-Nite Delivery, Boro-Cab, and Stronghold Sentries.

"I used to be All-Nite Delivery," Arthur said. "They've got a lot of brand names." Looking around, he said, "Just a minute, maybe on a side street." He turned onto Leroy Street and said, "There's my parking place, right up there. Cosmopolitan's got a lot of other companies and shells of companies tucked inside it," he went on. "Some of them act like they're completely independent, and some are empty, just brand names in case they happen to need something."

Arthur parked in the space he'd found, locked the Volvo, and they walked back down Hudson. On the way, he said, "I never had to know the corporate structure there. In fact, I always had the idea it was better for me *not* to know the corporate structure. My front job was with Cosmopolitan, over in Jersey, my checks came from Cosmopolitan on a Bayonne bank, and if I had a problem I called whoever they said I should call, and I kept my nose clean." He shrugged. "Lot of good it did me."

"You've been to this place before," Parker said.

"It used to be my office."

"What's the layout?"

"All the offices are upstairs," Arthur told him. "Receptionist, little room at the top of the stairs. Behind her, a center hall, offices on left and right. Left has those front windows. Mine was the last window up there on the left. That's where Rafe is now."

"We'll go up," Parker said. "You give your name and ask for Hargetty."

"Right."

Parker opened the street door, had Arthur go in first, and they headed up the stairs.

Some effort had been made to soften this fireproof iron-and-concrete stairwell, with beige carpeting and walls, plus framed nineteenth-century photographs of New York City street scenes; horse-drawn trolleys, slender distant women in black silhouette lifting their skirts out of the mud.

There was a dark wood railing at the top of the stairs, but no wall. Arthur stepped around the ornate newel at the end of the rail and Parker followed, seeing, against the rear wall, a thin middle-aged woman in thick black sweater and black-framed harlequin glasses seated behind a broad desk cluttered with phone and computer equipment, in-out baskets, packages of various kinds, phone books, small file boxes, a long Rolodex, and a variety of over-the-counter medicines. She was on the phone, nodding, not speaking, taking notes on a memo pad. She nodded at Arthur, wagged her pen briefly to assure him he was next, and went on listening and writing. Finally, she said, "I'll be sure he gets this as soon as he comes in. Yes, thank you. Thank you, you did the right thing."

One more nod and she hung up, then shook her head, said, "Phew," looked at the notes she'd made, shook her head again, pushed that pad to one side, and gave Arthur a bright look: "Yes, sir, good morning."

"Morning," Arthur said. "Rafe Hargetty in?"

Already reaching for the phone, she said, "Who shall I say?"

"Arthur Hembridge."

She dialed a two-digit number, waited briefly, said, "Mr. Hargetty, an Arthur Hembridge and another gentleman are here." She nodded, sending a little meaningless smile in Arthur's direction, then said, "I will," hung up, and said, "Mr. Hargetty will be right out. You could have a seat over there while you wait."

Across the room, under a window overlooking the street, were two sofas in an L, with a glass coffee table bearing half a dozen newspapers and magazines. As they crossed to it, Arthur said, "She's new. Well, it's been eight years."

Parker sat with the window behind him, the receptionist ahead of him across the room, Arthur on the other sofa to his left, the inner door to the offices beyond Arthur. The receptionist was now typing, interrupted from time to time by the telephone. She handled all these calls herself, making notes or asking questions, never transferring anyone to the people in the other offices.

They waited a little more than five minutes, and then that inner door opened and a man came out. Big-muscled but lean in torso, he looked like an oil-well driller in his wedding-and-funeral suit. Though he was probably in his mid-forties, his face and hands were weathered and lined, and he moved awkwardly, as though putting him indoors in city clothes had robbed him of both the self-assurance and balance he would have felt out on the rig.

His smile was awkward, too, as he came forward, big-knuckled hand out, saying, "Arthur! By God, it's been a hundred years!"

Arthur and Parker had both risen, and now Arthur stepped forward to accept the handshake, saying, "At least that long, Rafe. You look good."

"So do you," Rafe said, his questioning eye glancing off Parker.

Arthur said, "This is Mr. Parker, part of the reason I'm here."

Rafe winced at the name; a tiny movement, but Parker saw it. Turning, hand out again, Rafe said, "Mr. Parker, glad to know you. Any friend of Arthur's."

"You, too," Parker said, and they shook briefly, Rafe already looking away.

Rafe put his hands on his hips, arms akimbo, as though looking out over a cliff. That uneasy smile flickered again, and he said, "Well, Arthur, what can I do you for?"

Arthur's smile seemed very natural. "We'd like to have a little chat in your office, if you have a minute," he said.

"Well, sure," Rafe said, turning away. "Come on. *Your* office, too, you know."

"I imagine there've been changes," Arthur said.

"A few," Rafe agreed, and led the way down a func-

tional cream-colored hall with overhead fluorescents.
Most of the doors to both sides were open, most of the
small offices occupied, with one man or woman at a
desk, talking on the phone or staring at the computer.

The last office on the left, Rafe's, was just as small
and cramped as the rest. He went in first, shut the
door after them, and said, "Only one chair, there. Unless you want mine."

Parker stayed standing by the door. "The first thing
you can do, Rafe," he said, "is call Frank Meany back,
tell him—"

They both stared. Rafe said, *"What?"* as though he
didn't speak English.

"—Arthur got spooked by something," Parker went
on, "and left."

Arthur, saddened but not surprised, said to Rafe,
"You knew."

Deciding to tough it out, Rafe said, "I'm not sure
what you two—"

Parker showed him the pistol, without pointing it
anywhere; a Beretta Jetfire automatic in .25 calibre,
strong enough for indoors. "Call him now," he said,
"or you don't leave this room alive."

Arthur said, "Rafe, for God's sake—"

"No, Arthur," Parker said. "Rafe doesn't have time
for that. Meany's sending people right now." He took
a step closer to Rafe and raised the Beretta, because
only an eye-shot would be sure. "Phone now."

Rafe blinked at the pistol staring at him. "You can't
shoot a gun in here," he said.

Parker shot the front panel of the wooden desk. The flat sound swelled in the room, but wouldn't reach far beyond it. Parker lifted the Beretta toward Rafe's eye again.

The sound of the shot had broken something in Rafe, like a high note breaking glass. He became boneless, and dropped backward into his desk chair, still looking at the Beretta. Parker and Arthur watched him for one long second, and then Rafe shook his head, reached out, picked up the phone.

"Redial," Parker said.

Rafe blinked at him, thinking about that, then shrugged, with a bitter sound in his throat. "I'm not clever," he said, as though it were a failing that had long troubled him, and pushed redial.

Parker came around the desk to lean close, so he could hear both sides of the conversation.

The phone rang three times, and then a woman's voice answered, saying some company name that Parker didn't quite catch. Rafe said, "It's Rafe Hargetty again, let me talk to Frank."

"One moment."

Parker was close enough to smell a kind of metallic haze that rose from Rafe, as though he'd just been electrocuted. It was the smell of fear.

"Rafe?" A hard, fast, tough-guy voice. "*Keep* him there, I got people on the way, use—"

"He left, Frank."

"What? You said he was there."

"Him and another guy. They left before I got outside. I don't know, something spooked them."

"What's the other guy look like?"

"I never saw him, Frank." Rafe's fear came across as the underling's desperate desire to please. He said, "They were gone before I got out there."

"Shit," said the voice. "There's only one reason Arthur's off the reservation. Let me think."

They all let Frank think. Arthur stood glaring at Rafe with heavy anger, while Rafe stared at his desktop, eyes and mouth moving as though he still thought there was some way he could turn this around, even though he knew there was nothing in the world he was ready to try.

"Rafe. Rafe, you there?"

"Yeah, sure!"

"If he comes back— Who've you got there? Anybody could hold them?"

"There's always a few drivers downstairs," Rafe said, "but they already left, I don't think they're—"

"If they do," Frank interrupted. "If they do come back, don't call me first, call downstairs first, get your hands on little Arthur and whoever the other guy is, *then* call me."

"Okay, Frank."

"Which is what you shoulda done this time."

"I didn't think, I just wanted—"

"I know, Rafe. Maybe they'll give you a second chance."

"I'll—I'll take care of it, Frank. If they come back."

"Good," Meany said, and broke the connection.

Rafe hung up, and turned his troubled look on Arthur. "I'm sorry," he said.

"Sorry for what in particular, Rafe?"

"I'm not around violence, Arthur," Rafe said. "You know that, no more than you ever were."

Arthur shook his head. "You're around it now."

Parker said, "What's the link between Cosmopolitan and Paul Brock?"

Rafe had the scared reaction of somebody who's been falsely accused: *"Who?"*

Arthur said, "You don't know this fella Brock?"

"Never heard the name in my life," Rafe said, blinking at Arthur. "I'm not going to lie to you, Arthur, not now, not like this."

"If you don't know Brock," Arthur said, "what *do* you know?"

"Frank came to me, a little while ago," Rafe told him. "He knew you and me kept in touch, he wanted to call you, give you a job."

"A job," Arthur said.

Rafe looked at Parker, then down at his hands curled on the desktop. "I'm not proud of this," he told his hands.

"Bullshit, Rafe," Arthur said. "We do what's needed."

Not looking up from his hands, Rafe said, "He wanted me to know, in front, you weren't gonna come out of it. So I wouldn't have a complaint later, he told me the setup."

Arthur waited, looking at Rafe's bowed head. After

a minute, Rafe sighed, shook himself, and said, "What it was, there was a guy worked for Cosmopolitan, I guess a hit man, I don't know, and he did private jobs sometimes, too. He did a private job that got him killed, and Cosmopolitan didn't like it, they had a lot invested in the guy, and it looked bad if their pro got put down by some independent named Parker that nobody knew, so they took it over, the private job, they made it a Cosmopolitan job."

"My job," Arthur said.

"Yeah." Rafe looked up at Parker. "I don't know what you're gonna do to me, right now," he said, "but you got a whole big corporation looking to shut you down."

Parker pointed the Beretta at the memo pad on Rafe's desk. "Write down Frank Meany's addresses and phone numbers. Where he works and where he lives."

"I don't know where he lives," Rafe said, and at Parker's expression he said, "I swear to God!"

Arthur, quietly, said, "I never knew where Frank lived either."

"On the job, then," Parker said.

Rafe looked from one to the other, not saying he was dead no matter what he did now, because they all knew that. Then he made a sour face and said, "He's at Cosmopolitan, over in Bayonne."

Parker looked at Arthur. "You know the place?"

Shaking his head, Arthur said, "I used to know the address. I was never there."

Parker nodded at Rafe. "Write it down."

Obediently, Rafe picked up his pen and wrote the company name and address on the memo pad.

Parker said, "What does he do there?"

"PR," Rafe said.

Parker frowned. "What?"

"Public relations," Rafe explained. "He's head of public relations."

"That's the company's idea of a joke," Arthur said, picking up the whole pad, putting it in his jacket pocket. "That and bombs." Looking at Parker, he gestured toward Rafe: "Why won't he call Frank as soon as we leave?"

"Because," Parker said, "either I shoot him dead, or he comes with us. It's up to him."

Slowly, Rafe got to his feet.

7

West of the Holland Tunnel, the Turnpike Extension rides high over the Jersey flats, where garbage and construction debris and used Broadway sets and failed mobsters have been buried for a hundred years. Arthur drove, with Parker and Rafe behind him on the backseat. Rafe had nothing to say until Arthur took one of the steep twisty ramps down from the Extension into the industrial wasteland of the flats. Then, not looking at Parker, he said, "I'd like to live through this."

"Everybody would," Parker told him.

The street they took south was flanked by warehouses and vast parking fields full of tractor trailers. There were no pedestrians in this part of the world, and almost no other traffic. Parker said, "Arthur, how far?"

"Ten minutes."

"Pull over at the next cross street."

Rafe blinked, but wouldn't look at Parker.

As the Volvo slowed, Parker said to Rafe, "Take off your shoes and socks."

"I'm not trouble to anybody," Rafe said, still looking straight ahead. Then, when Parker didn't answer, he stooped to take off the shoes and socks, saying, "Just leave them on the floor?"

"Yes. Empty your pockets. Onto the floor."

Rafe did so, wallet and keys and coins and a penknife dropping down by his shoes.

Arthur had stopped the Volvo. Parker got out, on the curbside, and said, "Come out."

Rafe slid over and climbed out of the car. He looked very scared, and kept his eyes fixed on a point somewhere to Parker's right.

Parker said, "Walk somewhere."

Surprised he was going to stay alive, Rafe looked quickly at Parker's face, then down at his own bare feet, then started walking, stepping carefully, frowning down at the scarred broken concrete of the sidewalk.

Parker got into the front beside Arthur. "We'll be done before he calls anybody."

"Good," Arthur said. "I was afraid you wouldn't have an easy way." He put the car in gear and drove on south, Rafe picking his way slowly through the wasteland behind them.

It's called the Port of New York, but years ago most of the shipping businesses moved across the harbor to New Jersey, where the costs were lower and the regulations lighter. Newark, Elizabeth, Jersey City, and Bayonne are, along their waterfronts, a great sweeping tangle of piers, warehouses, gasoline storage towers, snaking rail lines, cranes, semi–tractor trailers, chain-link fences, guard shacks, and forklift trucks. Day and night, lights glare from the tops of tall poles and the corners of warehouses. Cargo ships ease up the channels and into the piers every hour of every day from every port in the world. The big trucks roll eastward from the Turnpike and the cargo planes lift from Newark International. The thousand thousand businesses here cover every need and every want known to man.

This was the home of Cosmopolitan Beverages, or at least the home of their legitimate business. On the roof of a broad three-story brick building a long time ago painted dull gray a sparkling red-and-gold neon sign read COSMOPOLITAN in flowing script and, beneath that, BEVERAGES in smaller red block letters. The building stood alone, surrounded by frost-heaved concrete patched here and there with asphalt. Between the expanse of concrete and the equally choppy street stretched a chain-link fence across the front of the property, turning at right angles at both ends to stretch back toward the piers and Upper New York Bay. Gates in both front corners stood open, the one on the left leading to a mostly full parking area beside the building, the one on the right opening to a smaller and mostly empty space, with a sign on the fence near the gate reading VISITOR PARKING.

Arthur turned in at the visitors' gate, saying, "Same as last time?"

"No. I'll be Hargetty." Parker looked at Arthur's profile as the older man stopped the car near the front corner of the building. "You have any guns in this car?"

Arthur shook his head. "I've never owned a gun in my life," he said. "Fired rifles, a long time ago, in the army. Only at targets."

"If it turns bad," Parker told him, "drop flat and roll into a corner."

"And consign my soul to Jesus."

"If you want."

They got out of the car. "Don't lock it," Parker said, since Arthur was about to.

"Right," Arthur said.

The old concrete surrounding the building was like broken ice on a lake after a thaw and refreeze, but slicing through it in a straight line from visitors' parking across the facade to the main front entrance was a four-foot-wide swatch of newer uncracked concrete. They took this walk, Parker going first, and inside the revolving door was a broad reception area, a wide low black desk on a shiny black floor, with no other furniture. The rear wall was curved, shiny silver, as though they were inside a platinum egg. On that wall were mounted, in a random pattern, bottles of the different liquors the company imported, each in its own clear plastic box; beside each was displayed that brand's Christmas gift box.

The receptionist was a black man, thin, thirtyish, with a thick brush of a moustache that made the face behind it seem slighter, less important. He wore jeans and a dark green polo shirt under a maroon blazer with CB in ornate gold letters on the pocket. He watched Parker and Arthur cross to him as though their existence were baffling but unimportant, as though the idea of "visitors" had never been tested here before.

Parker reached the desk and said, "Frank Meany."

The man nodded, nothing more.

Parker said, "We want to see him."

Finally the man had something to say: "Did you phone him?"

"Yeah, just a little while ago."

"And he said to come *here*?"

"He didn't say I was supposed to talk to you, he said I was supposed to talk with him."

The man looked around, as though there should be somebody else here to discuss this situation with, but then he shrugged and turned away, reaching for his phone.

Parker waited, watching him make an interior call. The man spoke softly, but could be heard: "Some people here for Mr. Meany." A little pause, and, "That's what they say." Another little pause, and, "I'll ask him." He turned to Parker: "Who are you?"

"Rafe Hargetty."

The man repeated the name into the phone, then said, "Okay," and sat back in his swivel chair, looking at nothing, tapping the eraser end of a pencil on his belt buckle.

Parker looked around. There was nothing in this reception area but the desk and the wall display and the indifferent man in his maroon Cosmopolitan jacket. There was no seating area for visitors, no magazines laid out. Cosmopolitan did make some effort to look like a normal business, but the effort was halfhearted. Possibly they didn't know that business visitors were normally given a place to sit and wait; certainly they didn't care.

In the silver wall, near the right corner, was an unobtrusive door, the same silver, which now opened and three men came out. Even before Arthur said, in a quick bark, "Frank," and the first one through the doorway frowned in this direction, Parker knew this must be Meany. He was tall and bulky, with a bruiser's round head of close-cropped hair that fists would slide off. He'd been dressed very carefully by a tailor, in a dark gray suit, plus pale blue dress shirt and pink-and-gold figured tie, to make him look less like a thug and more like a businessman, and it might have done a better job if the tailor'd been able to do something about that thick-jawed small-eyed face as well. The four heavy rings he wore, two on each hand, were not for decoration. He had a flat-footed walk, like a boxer coming out of his corner at the start of the round.

But the second man through the doorway drew Parker's attention almost as much. He was another thug, less imposing than Meany, dressed in chinos and blue workshirt with the sleeves rolled partway up. There were white bandages on his forehead, right ear, right cheek, and the backs of both hands. He was the guy who'd gone through Larry Lloyd's picture window.

Parker stepped closer to the desk, drawing the

Beretta, knowing it wasn't enough in this large space against three, but having nothing else. The bandaged thug was reaching toward his hip, and so was the third man, a carbon copy without the bandages. Arthur was backing away, startled, ready to drop and roll into a corner.

But Meany immediately held both arms out in front of himself, palms out, like a referee telling the teams the down is over. "Hold it!" he said, with the absolute assurance he'd be heard.

Everybody stopped. Parker waited to see what would happen, the Beretta just visible to them all above the desk.

Meany looked aside at his own people, to be sure they'd stopped, then looked at Parker and said, with impatience, "What are you gonna do with that Mattel toy? Give it to Norm, come on back to the office, we'll talk it over. You're Parker, aren't you?"

"Yes," Parker said.

"So we've got things to talk about," Meany told him, and the small eyes shifted. "Arthur, hello," he said. "You might not believe this, but I'm glad to see you walkin around. Come on back, let's talk this over." He looked again at Parker: "Well?"

"I'll keep the toy," Parker said, and put the Beretta away.

8

Behind the silver wall, the building was immediately a warehouse, long and broad, concrete-floored, pallets of boxes stacked nearly to the fluorescents hanging in garish white lines from the ten-foot ceiling. The space was full of the echoing sound of machinery, motors, some nearer, some farther off, all too loud for normal conversation.

Meany turned right, Arthur following, then Parker, then the other two. They walked past long wide aisles made by the stacks of boxes, with workmen and fork-lifts visible some distance away. At the last aisle, Meany turned left, and partway along there the stacks on the right were replaced by a concrete block interior wall, spotted with gray metal doors and square windows of plate glass.

They went past the first door and window, through which Parker saw four people seated at desks, working

on computers. The second door and window led to a
room with fax, copier, and storage, empty right now,
and Meany opened the third door, into what had to be
his office, functional but roomy.

Meany went in first, then Arthur, then Parker, who
stepped to his left. As the bandaged guy came in,
Parker took out the Beretta, stuck it against the guy's
ear, and fired. The sound was like a cough from a
lion's cage.

Before the body could fall, Parker stepped in to
clasp it around the chest with his left arm, while his
right hand dropped the Beretta on the floor and went
to that hip holster the guy had reached for earlier. He
came out with a snub-nosed .32, thumb finding the
safety, and stepped back, holding the body close, as
the others all turned to gape at him. Meany, disbeliev-
ing, cried, "What did you *do?*"

Parker said, "Arthur, get their guns. Stay out of the
line of fire."

Arthur, understanding he didn't have the luxury of
time to be shocked right now, gave a spastic nod and
said, "Right. Will do." His voice trembled, but he
moved.

Parker shut the door with his shoulder and leaned
against it, the body held against his chest, the .32
showing around the dead man's side. He watched
Meany, knowing the other guy wouldn't move without
instructions, and Meany watched him, with growing
anger, his face reddening. He didn't react when
Arthur patted him down, removing a pistol from be-

neath the well-tailored jacket, but kept staring at Parker.

Parker said, "Put the guns on the desk."

Arthur did, one pistol from each of them, and then Parker let the body fall, stepping away from it, saying, "Meany, put your hands on your head."

"Or what?" Meany's voice was strangled, his throat choked with rage.

"Or I gut-shoot you," Parker said, "and you live long enough to answer questions." He aimed the .32 just below Meany's belt buckle.

"You come in here," Meany said, furious about it, but putting his hands up, lacing his fingers atop his head, "you pull this against three of us, in the middle of our operation! How are you gonna get out of here?"

"That isn't your problem," Parker told him. "How *you* get out of here, that's your problem." Turning to the other one, he said, "Face down on the floor, over there, away from that chair. Clasp your hands at the back of your neck. Spread your feet apart. Farther." When the guy had obeyed orders, Parker said, "Arthur, use one of those guns. Just hold it on that guy down there. Don't shoot him unless he moves."

Arthur tried to pick up the gun as though it were something he did all the time. He moved Meany's telephone so he could rest his hand on it, pistol pointing at the man on the floor.

Parker said to Meany, "Brock and Rosenstein had a private grudge against me. You people dealt yourself in."

"You killed a valuable asset of ours," Meany said.

Parker nodded. He said, "How many assets you want to lose before you start to mind your own business?"

Meany couldn't believe it. "You're threatening *us*?"

"I'm nothing to do with you," Parker told him, "unless you push yourself into my face. Then I come here, and you start to lose assets."

Meany shook his head. "How long before you run out your string?"

"You think I'm here out of luck?" Parker stepped over to the man on the floor, went on one knee beside him, said, "Move your hands under your chin."

The guy did so, and Parker laid the tip of the barrel against the side of his neck toward the rear, gun parallel to the floor. Meany watched him, blinking, not knowing what was supposed to happen now.

Parker looked up at him, the gun held steady. He said, "You got a good health plan, here at Cosmopolitan?"

"What?" Meany was too bewildered now to remember to be outraged.

Parker said, "If I shoot this guy across the back of the neck here, just here, it doesn't kill him. All it does is break his spinal cord, leave him paralyzed the rest of his life. You people gonna support him, another forty, fifty years, in that wheelchair?"

"Jesus Christ," Meany said. The man on the floor was trembling, body rattling against the wood.

Parker stood. "But why do it to him? He's just a soldier. I do it to you, that means you're alive, you can tell your pals at Cosmopolitan how I can be rough on assets. Face down on the floor."

"You can't— Jesus—"

"*Down.* Or do I put out your knee first?"

Meany stared over at Arthur, as though for help, then squinted again at Parker. "Let's talk," he said.

9

Parker said, "There's no promise you can make me, nothing you can say. Cosmopolitan decided to come after me, Cosmopolitan has to decide to go away, so Cosmopolitan has to start hurting. On the floor."

"They can back off right now," Meany insisted. He was trying to hold his dignity together, to be urgent without showing panic. "We don't have to do anything else about you at all."

"Once I leave here," Parker told him, "if you're still an *asset*, you're gonna decide your pride is hurt, you'll want—"

"Not me, pal," Meany said. "You come in here like this, you shoot George in the head just, what? Just attract attention? *I'm* not gonna pick any fights with you, wonder when you're gonna find out where I live. Cosmopolitan is out of this, as of now."

Parker looked over at Arthur. "Can he make an offer like that?"

"I don't think so," Arthur said. "He's just a guy works here, like I used to."

"I'll carry the message," Meany said.

"Yes, you will," Parker agreed. "On the floor."

"I'll carry it now! I'll make a phone call!"

"Who to?"

Meany licked his lips. His elbows were twitching back and forth from the strain of holding his hands together on top of his head. "One of the owners," he said. "A guy that *can* make the offer."

"What's his name?"

Meany didn't like doing this, but knew he had no choice. "Joseph Albert."

Parker looked at Arthur. "Do you know that name?"

"I never knew any of the owners," Arthur said.

Meany said, "There's five guys have an interest in Cosmopolitan. Albert's the one I know, the one put me here."

"We'll try it," Parker decided, and glanced toward the window, with its view of the aisle and the stacked boxes. Sooner or later, someone would walk by out there. He said, "Arthur, get up and take a lace out of one of Meany's shoes."

"Right."

"You on the floor," Parker said, "get up."

The man scrambled to his feet, looking back and forth between Parker and Meany.

Parker said, "Move your friend against the wall under the window, then sit in that chair over there."

When the body was moved where Parker wanted, it couldn't be seen from the aisle outside. Parker turned back to Arthur, who now stood with a shoelace in his hand. "Good," he said. "Meany, put your hands in front of yourself like you're praying."

"I *am* praying," Meany said. He put his palms together.

Parker said, "Arthur, tie his thumbs together. Tight. Meany, is that a speakerphone?"

"Sure."

"Done," Arthur said, and stepped back from Meany.

There was one other chair in the room. Parker backed to it, saying, "Arthur, put the guns in the wastebasket. Meany, sit at the desk. Arthur, stand beside him and dial the phone. Copy down the number he calls."

Meany awkwardly fitted himself into his desk chair, cumbersome without the use of his hands. "Mr. Albert isn't gonna like this," he said.

"Tell Arthur the number."

It was a Manhattan area code. Arthur wrote it on Meany's desk pad, then pressed the speakerphone button and dialed. They all listened to two rings, and then a woman's voice said, "Enterprises, good afternoon."

"Mr. Albert, please."

"Who shall I say is calling?"

"Frank Meany."

"One moment."

Enterprises' on-hold music was Vivaldi. Through it,

Meany said to Parker, "Saying things on the phone isn't easy. You know what I mean, anybody listening in."

"You'll figure it out," Parker said.

"I'm motivated, you mean," Meany said.

They listened to Vivaldi for four minutes. Then the woman came back on the line to say, "Mr. Meany?"

"Yeah."

"If you're in the office, Mr. Albert will call you back in ten minutes."

"Now," Parker said, and the woman, confused, said, "What?"

"Tell Mr. Albert," Meany said, "it's kind of urgent. He can talk to me from right there."

"One moment."

Vivaldi again. Meany, apologetic, said, "He was going to another phone. You know, so it wouldn't be in the office."

"I'm not gonna spend much more time here," Parker said.

Meany looked down at his tied-together thumbs. "I'm calling him," he said. "I'm doing all I can do."

Vivaldi answered him, for another half-minute, and then a new voice, heavy, guarded, came on, saying, "Frank?"

"Hello, Mr. Albert." Meany sounded nervous in a different way now. Parker was an immediate lethal problem, Mr. Albert a longer-term problem, maybe also lethal. "I'm sorry to interrupt you," he said, "but I got a decision to make, and I need your okay."

"What decision?"

"Well, sir," Meany said, hunched forward over his praying hands while small lines of perspiration ran down either side of his face, "you remember we had an arrangement with a Mr. Parker after we stopped dealing with Mr. Charov."

There was a little pause, and then, "That's right," Mr. Albert said.

"Well, Mr. Parker's here with me now," Meany said, "in the office, and he'd like to end the arrangement, you know, just not have a relationship with Cosmopolitan at all any more, and I told him I thought that was the right thing to do, but we both know I got to get an okay from higher up, so he thought I should call you, and I thought that was a good idea."

Mr. Albert said, "He's there with you now?"

"Yes, sir."

Parker said, "On the speakerphone."

"Ah," Mr. Albert said.

Parker said, "If you want, I could finish up with Frank here and come discuss it with you personally."

"No, I don't think— I don't think that would be necessary, Mr. Parker."

"But the other thing is," Parker said, "I'll need some way to get in touch with Paul Brock. I mean, if you and I are finished with one another, then that just leaves the Paul Brock situation, and I think I ought to deal with that myself. Not put you people to any more effort."

There was a little pause, and Mr. Albert said, "Paul Brock is a valuable asset to our company, Mr. Parker."

"I understand that," Parker said. "Like Frank here."

"Ah. What it comes down to is, I have a choice to make."

Parker waited. Meany said, "I think Mr. Parker's way is gonna work out best for us, Mr. Albert."

"On balance," Mr. Albert said, "I believe you're right. So Mr. Parker needs a way to get in touch with Brock."

Parker said, "Yeah, I need that."

"Frank, you go ahead and give Mr. Parker Brock's address. I don't believe I have it here myself."

"Okay, Mr. Albert," Meany said.

Parker leaned a little closer to the phone. He said, "But you do go along with Frank's idea here, that we don't have any more business together."

"Happily," Mr. Albert said. "To be honest, I always felt it was a diversification we shouldn't have gone into. We let . . . a certain proprietary sense cloud our judgment."

"Everybody makes mistakes," Parker said.

"Well, I'm happy we have the opportunity to correct this one," Mr. Albert said. "Frank, is there anything else?"

"No, sir," Meany said, eager to get this finished, now that it seemed to be working out. "Just needed your okay to end the arrangement with Mr. Parker."

"It's ended. Goodbye, Mr. Parker," Mr. Albert said, and the dial tone sounded until Arthur found the button to switch off the speakerphone.

10

Parker said, "Arthur, write Brock's address on the same sheet as that phone number."

"You can trust Mr. Albert," Meany said.

Parker waited.

Meany turned to Arthur. "Brock and Rosenstein are over in New York, in Greenwich Village. It's four-one-four Bleecker."

As Arthur wrote that down, Parker said, "Brock hired Charov for his own personal reason, but Brock was already connected here."

"He's like a supplier," Meany said. "He doesn't work regular for us."

"But he's another valuable asset. What makes him valuable?"

"You don't know?" Meany was surprised. "Electronics. He does all our debugging, all the phone lines in all our operations, comes through on a regular basis, like the exterminator. And specialty stuff. He made those bombs, set that up."

Parker nodded. "Gave you people one more reason to help him get rid of me."

Meany shrugged. "Seemed like it ought to be easy."

Arthur said, "Is Albert going to warn Brock we're coming?"

"No," Meany said. "We want no more of this. If Mr. Albert calls Brock, and Parker finds out about it, here he comes again."

"No," Parker said. "I'd go see Albert."

"He knows that, too," Meany said.

Parker got to his feet, put the .32 away in his pocket, picked the Beretta off the floor. "You two walk us out to the car," he said.

Meany held up his hands. "Still like this?"

"I don't need you to wave goodbye," Parker said. "Come along."

On Sixth Avenue, just into Manhattan from the Holland Tunnel, Parker said, "Let me off here."

Surprised, Arthur said, "Aren't I coming with you?"

"Not needed."

"Oh. Okay."

Arthur pulled to the curb by a fire hydrant. "I was getting used to going places with you," he said.

"Now you're retired again," Parker told him, and got out of the Volvo. A block north, at a pay phone, he called Lloyd at home in Massachusetts: "Tell the others, I'm finishing up here, I'll see them out there day after tomorrow."

"Good," Lloyd said. "You're all done there?"

"One last detail," Parker said.

THREE

1

Horace Griffith was in Geneva, negotiating the sale of a Titian, when the e came from Paxton Marino: "Need to talk to you soonest. Give me a number I can call."

Paxton Marino was a very good customer of Griffith's, a dot-com nouveau riche who judged his happiness level by how fast he could spend his money, but he was also a difficult and a cranky customer—a spoiled brat, in fact—who had already caused Griffith more gray hairs than he could afford at fifty-six.

Still, the art market was always changeable and fraught with potential disaster, so it was good to have a cash cow the size of Paxton Marino still on the string. Because of that, Griffith did no more than sigh just the once before replying with the name and number of the Geneva hotel.

It was seven minutes later that the phone rang; Marino must have been more anxious to spend than

usual. It was 9:30 in the morning here; Griffith wondered where Marino was phoning from.

"I'm in New York," Marino said, by way of hello. "If
you're in Geneva, I'll fly over today, we can have dinner at my place in Courmayeur."

"Sounds urgent," Griffith said. He didn't mention
that Marino also sounded nervous, rattled, something
Griffith had never experienced with the man before.

"No no," Marino said, "not urgent," belying the
words with the manner in which they were said. "Just
a chat, that's all, a little chat over dinner."

I can drive down after lunch, get there before dark,
Griffith thought, and said, "It will be wonderful to see
you again, Pax."

"You, too," Marino said, in a hurry, and hung up.

Weird, Griffith thought. To sound upset like that, to
make a phone call at what had to be three-thirty in the
morning his time, not to take ten minutes to describe
all his latest acquisitions, to rush across the Atlantic
merely for dinner and a "chat"?

And Marino would have to open the house in Courmayeur, too, because this was far too early for the season there. It wasn't till December that the rich
Milanese would come up to open their winter chalets
high in the Italian Alps. Paxton Marino would never
be caught dead at any of his residences in the off-
season; what was going on?

                    *   *   *

The three-hour drive would have been a little shorter for a European, but Griffith, being an American, had to show his passport twice after getting onto the Route Blanche outside Geneva; first when crossing into France to reach the northern end of the Mont Blanc Tunnel at Chamonix, the second when emerging from the seven-and-a-quarter-mile tunnel into Italy near Courmayeur.

The tunnel itself, repaired now after the grim 1999 fire that had incinerated thirty-nine people, seemed brighter than before, larger, even cleaner, and much more free of the big trucks that always used to give a sense of menace to this tube through the mountain, but Griffith couldn't escape a faint sense of ghosts hovering just beneath the rounded roof, a trembling memory of all those screams, the awareness of just how dark this burrow inside the Alps would be without electric lights.

Griffith didn't actually believe in ghosts, and yet he was always among them. He traded mostly in European paintings and sculpture, from the fourteenth to the eighteenth centuries, and most of the creators of those works had firmly believed in an unseen world, in spirits, in an often vengeful and occasionally merciful God. They'd painted saints and sinners, martyrs and miracles, and Griffith had steeped himself in their work.

He had also, in the darker side of his profession, showed himself to be at one with the world those artists had described. He, too, was merely human, full of error. He didn't really believe in all that cosmic moral accounting, but he couldn't help some faint awareness in the back of his mind that, if retribution ever did fall on him, he'd damn well deserve it.

Every dealer in valuable art, at a certain upper level of market worth, is offered the temptation now and again. To deal, in almost absolute safety, with stolen work, or forged work. Griffith at times envied those who had never fallen, but he also knew he could not possibly live as well, as comfortably, if he had been one of the virtuous ones. If virtue truly is its own reward, then Griffith regretfully had to go where the rewards were more palpable.

And if he'd remained a good boy, he'd never have known Paxton Marino, would he? Never have filled the amazingly lucrative position of being Marino's exclusive art agent, both in the legitimate deals . . . and in the others.

After the Italian checkpoint at the southern terminus of the tunnel, Griffith turned his rented Audi toward the town. All around, the chalets scattered along the slopes of the Val d'Aosta like spilled Monopoly houses looked bare and solitary against the scruffy treeless ground, without their usual luxury coats of snow. A little farther up, the snow never left the rocky land completely, not even with the warming of the globe, and up there was where Griffith was now headed.

Marino's ski chalet, built by him four years ago, lay north of the main resort, on the upslope fringe of

Dolonne. From its main living room, on the west side of the house, the cable cars could be watched, floating upward like tiny toys toward Checruit.

It wasn't the season yet for the cable cars. Empty, the black lines angled upward, off to his left, against a powder blue sky as cold as space. The Audi growled upward along the narrow road, happy with the challenge. Other traffic was sparse, mostly workers getting the chalets ready for the season.

Marino's house was, for him, modest, a gleaming white concrete structure cantilevered westward over a steep slope, its western and southern faces banks of plate glass edged in chrome. The drive curved upward beneath the house, so that swimmers in the glass-bottomed indoor pool could watch arrivals down through the heated water and the greenish glass.

The entry drive curled around the blank white north side of the house, facing the mountain, and ended at the east face, where the house met the land. Two staffmen were waiting outside the elaborate antique door, once part of a Landsruhe church, the only touch of wood on the facade of the house, one to take his luggage, the other to drive the Audi away to the garage.

Griffith followed the staffman into the house, enjoying again the icy luxury, the sense of imperious control, that characterized all of Marino's houses. He was led to the guest room where he'd stayed the other three times he'd been here; the staff would have records of things like that.

Putting his small suitcase on the bed, the staffman said, "Mr. Marino will see you at seven. He has not yet arrived."

"Thank you."

"If you wish to swim—"

"Thank you, I know where it is. And I brought my suit."

In the pool, Griffith saw the white Daimler arrive, tiny and toylike far below through the water and glass. (The pool was always disconcerting, but always a kick, too.) He was alone in the echoing and always faintly steamy swimming pool room, and he dove down to watch the Daimler disappear around the corner of the house, then surfaced again.

Because Griffith traveled among people who wined and dined very well indeed, he worked hard to keep himself in shape, with a small gym and lap pool at home in Dallas. Whenever while traveling he had an opportunity to swim laps he took it, staying in his lane even when the pool was as large and broad and empty as this one.

Now, he sliced through the water for just three more laps—sixty—then climbed out, dried himself, put on the sandals he'd found in the guest room closet, and rode the small elevator up one floor, then walked the wide hall to his room. The clock on the bedside table read 6:43. He dressed, took his evening pills—high blood pressure, high cholesterol—and walked back along the hall to the broad living room,

with its wonderful views west and south over the town
of Courmayeur and all the other villas and villages nestled in the folds of the mountain's skirt.

Marino wasn't here yet. Griffith accepted a Glenfid-
dich neat from the hovering staffwoman, and was
standing in front of the view, swirling the drink in his
mouth and the glass, when Marino arrived.

"Horace!"

Griffith turned, seeing his host cross toward him,
hand outstretched: "Pax," he said, and accepted the
firm handshake.

And knew at once that something wasn't right. The
urbane and calmly arrogant Paxton Marino he was
used to wasn't here; in his place was an uncertain man,
trying to hide his vulnerability. "Glad you could come,
Horace," he said. "I had them fly up steaks from
Rome, so we won't starve."

"Good."

Marino looked around for the staffwoman, saying,
"Do you have a— Oh, you have a drink."

"Yes." In negotiation, Griffith was known to be direct, sometimes unsettlingly so, and he sensed he was
in negotiation right now. "Pax," he said, making face
and voice only concerned as a friend would be, "what's
wrong?"

Marino flashed something like his normal smile.
"Wrong? Why should anything—" He broke off, with a
different smile, and a headshake. "Why do I waste
time trying to snow you? Sit down, sit down." Turning

away, he said to the staffwoman, "A Pellegrino, Helga, and then we'll be fine." Meaning she should go away.

Griffith took one of the low soft swivel chairs near the windows, as instructed, but once Marino got his glass of Italian water and Helga had padded away he remained on his feet, standing near Griffith but not looking at him, gazing at the valley out there instead.

Griffith watched and waited. Marino was thought of as a handsome man, but really was not, as Griffith now noticed for the first time. What was seen as handsomeness was merely self-assurance, a cockiness of stance, a smiling confidence that the world belonged to him. Take away that assurance—which something had done, that much was clear—and what was left was a tall but pudgy man in his mid-thirties. With his puffy cheeks like a squirrel, and slack body, and contact lenses that flashed the light more than he knew, Marino at last looked like what he actually was: a bright but uncharismatic science major out of the California state university system, a Fresno boy whose past was pizza and skateboards, not the Alps.

And not Horace Griffith. Like Marino, Griffith gazed out at the magnificent view. He wondered if Marino, too, might be thinking this was the last time either of them would see it.

At last Marino spoke: "You know, Horace, they keep saying the new economy's going bust."

"Yes, they do."

"It isn't, of course." Marino glowered out at the day as though daring it to disagree. "It has growing pains, that's all, maybe even birth pangs. But the doomsayers keep coming on and coming on, and here and there what they create is a self-fulfilling prophecy."

"I suppose so," Griffith said, wondering just how deep the hole was that Marino found himself in, and what the man expected Horace Griffith to do about it.

"I am watched like a hawk," Marino said. "You know that, Horace. I spend my money, I enjoy my money, I don't keep a low profile."

"No, you don't."

"So, when I run into a cash-flow problem—"

"Ah."

"That's all it is," Marino insisted, turning his glower at last full on Griffith. Still standing there in all that Alpine light, he looked like a later Roman emperor, lesser and more effete, but still both powerful and dangerous. "I have a cash-flow problem," he said. "It's temporary. I'm projected to be out of it in less than eighteen months, probably under a year. But the problem is, if I'm seen to cut back *anywhere*, it will be taken as a sign."

"Yes, of course."

"That's where the self-fulfilling prophecy comes in," Marino said. "With the hyenas. With the schadenfreude."

"We have that always with us," Griffith said.

"Of course we do." Marino waved that away. "I have a certain image. If the stockholders—if the Street generally—sees me tightening my belt, even a little bit, it could start a run. Not a logical sensible run, an irrational run that could nevertheless destroy me."

Marino drank a third of his Pellegrino, looked at it with a frown as though wishing now he'd asked for something stronger, and at last sat down, opposite Griffith, so that when they swiveled toward each other their profiles were to the view.

"Here's the situation I'm in," Marino said. "I have to either slow my spending awhile or sell off some of my property. Either choice is a bad one, sending a bad message."

"God, Pax," Griffith said. "You're in a hell of a situation here."

"I know that." Marino turned his head to look out at the view, reconsidered, faced Griffith again. "It finally occurred to me," he said, "I could get out from under all this if I sold off assets nobody knows I have."

Griffith instantly knew where Marino was going. The paintings, of course, hidden away beneath the lodge in Montana.

Griffith and Marino had been doing business together three or four years, Griffith happy with this freewheeling spender who did have a natural flair and some education as a collector, and who was flattering in his attention to Griffith's occasional advice, when this other side of their relationship first was broached. "There are paintings I'd love to own," Marino had said, in his hotel suite in London one evening after he and Griffith had attended a Sotheby's auction where Marino had been outbid twice but had managed three times to buy the pictures he'd wanted. "Paintings I'd love to own but I'll never get my hands on, and it just annoys me."

"Why won't you?" Griffith had asked.

"Because they aren't for sale. Either they're in museums, or they're in collections that will never come on the market."

"We all have our impossible dreams," Griffith had said, still thinking this was a theoretical conversation, not yet understanding where Marino was headed.

Which the man had next made clear: "Sometimes, though," he'd said, "paintings like that get stolen, and nobody ever sees them again. Except the thief, of course, or whoever the thief sold them to."

"I suppose so," Griffith had agreed, thinking of the Mona Lisa, the most famous of such thefts, and even now, so many years after the recovery, the continuing doubt that the version in the Louvre was the original.

"If a thief sold *me* a treasure like that," Marino had gone on, "you can be sure I'd never say a word about it." Laughing, he'd said, "Not that I'd ever deal with a thief, not directly, but if *you* brought me something like that, I'd certainly trust *you*."

And that was where it had started. Griffith already did have contacts in that other shady world, had made dubious sales for dubious people, had a few times acted as go-between in deals involving thieves and insurance companies, and Marino, as it turned out, really did have a wish list. In the last few years, they hadn't completely checked off every item on that list, but they'd done very well.

And Griffith himself had done very well in the process, knowing all along that in this arrangement he had taken one irrevocable step farther into the dark side than ever before. In the past, he had knowingly traded stolen property, he had knowingly represented forged property, but had never *commissioned* theft. On Paxton Marino's behalf, that's exactly what he'd now done. It had been risky, it had been nerve-wracking, it had cost him sleepless nights, but that's what he'd done.

And now, somehow, it was to be undone. Griffith all at once felt very weary, as though he'd been rolling some boulder up a mountain all his life, only to discover at this late date it was the wrong boulder. On the wrong mountain. He said, "Pax, you can't just sell those paintings."

"Oh, I know that." Marino, always a restless man, swiveled back and forth in his chair. "A couple months ago," he said, "we had a robbery at the lodge. They didn't get anything, thank God, and we got the thieves, or some of them, but they *found the gallery*."

That news gave Griffith a sudden chill. He'd only agreed to go along with this mad magpie instinct in Marino because the paintings would disappear forever, would never be seen in the normal world again. He said, "So they know? Not the law." Meaning, or we'd both be in jail already.

"No," Marino said, "the thieves don't seem to know

what they stumbled on. They've been questioned pretty thoroughly, and they're the kinds of people who wouldn't know a Rembrandt from an Elvis on velvet. But the point is, after we got the mess cleaned up, the mess they made going in, and after we added more security measures, *expensive* I might say security measures, this other thing came up, the realization I shouldn't be spending more than usual, I should be spending less than usual. Or liquidating a few assets, to tide me over. And I thought, there are crooks out there, they know there's *something* in that place, in the lodge, and a couple of them got away. I don't expect them to come back, but who knows, they could spread the story, go to prison for some other crime, tell their friends on the inside. So I was thinking I should move them anyway, sooner or later, and then it came to me, why not sell *off* some of them? Solve this temporary problem that way, at the same time I'm protecting myself against the crooks."

Griffith's glass was empty, but he felt he shouldn't ask for more. He said, "What do you want me to do, Pax?"

"You must have a list of them," Marino said. "The things I've got stashed out there."

"In code," Griffith said.

"Well, sure, in code. The thing is, choose three or four of them, your choice, whichever ones you think would be easiest to move. Go to the insurance companies, the museums, wherever. Say the thieves have been in touch with you." Then Marino stopped, sat back, gave a surprised laugh. "Which they have been, in a way, haven't they?" he said.

"You want me to negotiate on your behalf," Griffith said, "as though you're the thieves who took the paintings in the first place."

"That's right. In the meantime, I want you to go to the lodge, pack them all up—I can't trust *that* to anyone else—get them ready to go. Because this is the other part of it."

When Marino leaned closer to him like that, eyes intense, Griffith understood there was more to come, and that what was to come would be even worse.

Marino said, "What I'd like to do, Horace, is ship them all to you in Dallas as though they were just minor paintings, no importance at all, and you can store them in a normal way. Then, when the time comes to turn a few over to an insurance company or a museum, you've already got them."

Griffith swallowed. "And the rest?"

"Eventually," Marino said, as though it were all simple and casual, "you'll ship them to wherever I set up a new gallery."

"In the meantime, I hold on to them."

"Sure."

Millions of dollars of stolen artwork, in my vaults, Griffith thought. Famous paintings that any professional would recognize at once, stored in the safe rooms under my display space. I am suddenly deeper into this darkness than I've ever been before. But what can I do? I can't refuse. I got here by easy stages. Very easy stages.

Marino gave him a keen look, and then smiled, feeling better because Griffith was feeling worse. "I know," Horace," he said. "Life is gonna get tricky for both of us for a while. But it's going to come out okay. We've got the touch, you and me. This is a little patch of rough road, and then it's smooth again."

"Smooth," echoed Griffith.

Standing, Marino said, "Give me your glass, you need a refill. Then let's see what's happening with those steaks. I'm starved."

2

Pam Saugherty carried the ice cream and the milk in a plastic bag. D'Agostino's would deliver the rest of the groceries in half an hour or so. She crossed Abingdon Square, turned right onto Bleecker Street, and did one of those sidewalk dances with a man coming the other way, both of them moving to her left, then both reversing, then he stopping dead so she could choose for herself how to go around him.

"Excuse me," she murmured, with an embarrassed smile, knowing it was her fault. He nodded, not quite looking at her, and walked on.

She'd gone another five or six steps when his face became familiar. She'd seen that face before, bony, large, the eyes cold and uninterested, the jawline like a rock. She looked back and he was crossing the street at a diagonal, tall, big-boned, dressed in black, moving with a determined stride that made her surprised now he hadn't merely walked on over her when she'd gotten in his way. He strode around the corner into Bank Street, and out of sight, and Pam turned back toward home, frowning, weighed down much more by the elusive memory than by the plastic sack.

She knew that face. Reaching 414, she unlocked the street door, then paused to look back, across the street, at that corner of Bank Street. Something menacing in the memory, something frightening.

The mail had been delivered while she was out, pushed through the slot in the outer door onto the floor inside. Letting the door snick shut, she stooped to pick up the mail, mostly bills and catalogues, then unlocked the inner door.

It was the sight of the wheelchair that brought him back. The wheelchair to the left of the staircase that Matt so seldom used these days, the track for the riding chair built into the right side of the stairs for those rare trips Matt did take to the outside world. Seeing them both reminded her at last of the man, and the only time she'd ever seen him before, a time she usually managed not to think about at all.

Years ago, a hundred years it seemed, in another life, another world. The kids had still just been kids then, Bob, the oldest, only ten. She'd been married to Ed Saugherty, who had a good white-collar job with a computer company in Philadelphia, and they'd lived in a good brick house in a green suburb west of the city.

But Ed had a wild friend from his high school days,

a man named George Uhl, who had brought trouble
into the house, in himself and in a suitcase that had to
have had something valuable in it, though nobody
would ever find it now. Because Uhl was dead, and
these other two, Paul Brock and Matt Rosenstein, had
invaded the house, looking for the suitcase.

Matt intended to rape her, soon after they broke in,
and when Ed tried to stop him Matt turned on him,
beating him with a cold violence that was terrifying.
The other one, Paul Brock, had tried to stop Matt, but
he couldn't be stopped, until poor Ed was beaten into
a dead thing on the floor. Then Matt had done what
he wanted with Pam, and kept her and the children
tied and gagged in their bedrooms while they waited
for Uhl or the suitcase or whatever it was they wanted.

That part had seemed to go on forever, and only
ended when another man broke in, even faster and
harder than Matt. He'd shot both Matt and Paul,
knocking Paul down the basement stairs. Then he had
come in to where Pam was imprisoned, and untied
her, without softness or sympathy, just methodical, un-
caring, and saying only the one thing to her, once her
hands and mouth were free: "You know what to do."
Then he was gone.

She knew what he'd expected her to do, and what
at first she'd expected of herself as well. Revenge herself on Matt Rosenstein to begin with, somehow, some
painful way. Then call the police to come take this filth
out of here, out of her house, so she could get back to

the person she'd been before they'd invaded her world.

But there was no getting back. Ed was dead, and nothing would change that. She had seen evil, and been subjected to its whims, and nothing would ever let her forget that.

When, wearing nothing but the robe she'd just pulled on after the man had freed her, Pam had moved through this alien war zone that had once been her house, the first thing she'd found was Matt unconscious on the living room floor, near the kitchen doorway, a bloody gash on his forehead. And next was Paul, conscious but hurt, on his back on the basement floor, at the foot of the stairs.

She'd gone down those stairs, and Paul had called, his voice as faint as though it were coming from deep in a tunnel, "Help me!"

"*Help* you!" Rage caught at her and she loomed over him, ready to kill, ready to maim, wanting revenge on these terrible people.

But he stared up at her, meeting her eye, gasping, "I tried to stop him! You know I did, I tried to stop him, but I never could! Is he . . . alive?"

"I don't know," she said, reluctant, but having to answer, drawn by the intensity of his stare.

"Parker said his back was broken. Is he in pain?"

"He isn't conscious. He has a cut on his head."

"Oh, don't let him die!" Brock pleaded, and started to cry. "I know we don't deserve it, I know it's terrible, it's all gone so wrong, but please don't let him die!"

Baffled, caught by him despite herself, she'd said, "But . . . you're hurt, too. What about you?"

"I love him!"

She'd recoiled from that wail, and she recoiled now in memory, then started up the stairs, carrying the mail and the grocery bag, remembering that strange conversation in the basement of the house outside Philadelphia.

All Brock had cared about was his love for Matt Rosenstein. The intensity of it, the nakedness of it, even the selflessness of it, had cut through her anger, her need for revenge, her natural revulsion at the kind of love Brock was revealing to her.

But what to do? What could be done?

"I'll pay," Brock promised. "Keep Matt alive, I swear to you, I'll pay you whatever you need, I'll pay for your children, I'll pay for everything, only keep Matt alive!"

Her husband was dead. There was almost no insurance, she was a housewife with three children and no work history, no marketable skills. Rosenstein had been horrible, brutal beyond belief, but Brock had never been cruel, had tried to stop Rosenstein, had shown her decency in the middle of the horror. Now the reality of her situation pressed in on her while she listened to him, but what could she do? Rosenstein was unconscious up there, maybe dead already.

"There's a doctor I know," Brock told her. "Get me a phone, I'll call him, he'll take care of things."

The pity she felt was as much for herself as for him. Unwillingly, she said, "I could call an ambulance."

"No! That means police, jail, I'll never see Matt again in my life! This doctor, *he'll* help."

At the head of the stairs, she turned into the dining room, dropped the mail on the table there, turned toward the kitchen at the front of the house. From the bedroom at the back she could hear the television, Matt watching his soap operas. After she put the ice cream and milk away, she went back there, pushed open the door, saw Matt asleep in his wheelchair in front of the set.

Matt slept a lot these days, increasingly so over the years, never adapting himself to the reality of his paralysis, never trying to fight back, to become somebody new. Now he was a poor bloated creature, like something deep in a cave, so bitter and so sorry for himself there was no room for anyone else to feel sorry for him.

Pam's hatred for Matt, her desire for revenge, had faded a long time ago, but she would never be able to feel anything but repugnance for him as he was now. She knew that only the paralysis kept him from being the same cruel arrogant bastard he'd been years ago, when he'd first broken into her house. The only good thing about Matt Rosenstein, now or in the past or ever, was Paul Brock, and they all knew it.

She left Matt there asleep in front of his soap opera, and went on upstairs. The top floor was Paul's, his living room and bedroom and workshop, but the floor between was hers. Since the kids had gone off to college, one of their former bedrooms had become a sitting room for her, with her own TV, which she rarely watched. She listened to music there now, and read an English novel, and waited for dinnertime.

The man's name was Parker.

Dinner was usually the only part of the day when all three were together. Pam cooked and Paul came home from his shop to wheel Matt out to his place at the table. Matt could move his arms, though nothing below them, so he could feed himself. Usually he glowered at his plate and ate sloppily and had little to say, while Paul and Pam kept up the conversation. Paul was a slight man, under medium height, very thin, with a kind of friendly Ichabod Crane face. He wore heavy horn-rimmed glasses that made his eyes look huge.

Tonight, Pam had to tell them both about that strange meeting on the street. Once all three were at the table, she said, not looking at either of them in particular, "The man who came into my house that time, the man who shot you, I saw him today."

That drew an astounded silence. Paul stared at her, and even Matt roused himself to blink in her direction. And finally, Paul said, "You *saw* him? Where?"

"Out front. He was walking up the street, he turned onto Bank."

Paul took off his glasses and rubbed his eyes. The hand holding the glasses shook. "He's here," he said. "He found us."

"This is *you*, goddamit," Matt told him. His voice

rumbled now, and wheezed, from all the extra weight. Glaring at Paul, he said, "*You* fucked it up again, god-damit!"

"Charov was supposed to—"

"Charov!" Matt pounded his wheelchair arm. "Fucking Russian wasn't as good as he thought he was! None of you fucking people— If *I* could do something!"

"I have to call them," Paul said, and jumped up, and ran upstairs to make the call where Pam wouldn't hear it.

There were always things Paul had to keep from her, both in how he made his money and how he spent his evenings when he dressed up and went out smelling of cologne, and she was happy to be kept in the dark. She didn't want to know. His electronics shop on Fourteenth Street made a profit, but she knew that wasn't his real income, that wouldn't pay for this house or all the money he'd spent on her and her family over the years.

Matt turned his heavy glower in her direction, while she listened to the murmur of Paul on the phone upstairs. "A fat lot of help *you'll* be," he grumbled.

"I've been of help in the past," she told him. "I've been of help to *you.*" She didn't have to put up with his bad temper.

Matt had nothing more to say, and neither did she. Picking up her fork, she tried to eat, listening to the sounds of Paul from upstairs, then his footsteps hurrying back down.

He was white when he came into the room. He

didn't sit at his place at the table, but just stood there, barely beyond the doorway, staring with a horrified expression at Matt. "They cut us off."

Matt lifted his head. "What? They can't do that!"

"They did it." Paul seemed distracted, despairing, bewildered. "He went to them, he did something, I don't know what. They won't help any more. They told Parker they were out of it!"

"*Told* him!" Matt pounded the wheelchair arm. "Get me a gun! This time it's *my* turn, goddamit! Get me a gun!"

"Matt—"

Pam said, quietly, "Paul. If you give Matt a gun, I'm leaving."

"Goddam *bitch*!"

"That's all right, Matt," Paul said, and started to pat his shoulder, then realized this wasn't the time to get within arm's reach. Standing just far enough away, he said, "You don't need a gun, Matt. We'll figure this out. Don't worry, baby, he won't get in here. We'll figure it out."

3

At home, Frank Elkins and Ralph Wiss were completely different from the roles they played on the road. At home, they were family men, living not far from each other in the same Chicago suburb, involving themselves with their families and their community. They both had large extended families, several children each, and cousins and in-laws in all directions, but not one of those people knew what Elkins and Wiss really did for a living, except their wives. The two were known to work together, to travel a lot, and to bring home enough for a comfortable income, but that was all. "We do specialty promotions," Elkins would say, if pressed, as they rarely were, and Wiss would nod. They did specialty promotions.

Elkins considered himself very lucky, both in his family and in his partner. A lot of the guys he knew were loners, and didn't have much joy in their lives;

that wasn't him. As for the partner, it was Ralph Wiss who had the expertise, the craft. Elkins was just along to do the heavy lifting. Wiss was the one who knew safes and vaults, how they were locked, how they could be opened. Wiss did the brain work; once the door was breached, all Elkins had to do was pick up the contents and carry it home.

The Montana job had seemed made to order for them. There were clever locks for Wiss to play with, and a lot of heavy lifting. Too much for just the two of them, which was why they'd brought in Corbett and Dolan. Harry Corbett and Bob Dolan were younger than Elkins and Wiss, but both had been inside and had learned caution. Elkins and Wiss had worked with them in the past, and there'd never been any problem.

Now, there was a problem. Corbett and Dolan were ready to skip, start again with new names and new faces, but that took money. And they, too, had families, and it was their families who had put up the heavy bail money. If Corbett and Dolan couldn't make their families whole again on the bail, with enough left over for themselves, they'd have no choice but to stay and do the time. But that meant they'd also have no choice but to trade Elkins and Wiss for a shortening of that time.

It put a pressure on Elkins that he didn't like, but he couldn't see any way around it. If he were in Corbett and Dolan's shoes, he'd make the same offer. Nothing personal, just the physics of the situation.

The original message, with these alternatives, had been delivered through cutouts, Corbett and Dolan giving the word in a taped and sealed envelope to a friend who didn't know Wiss or Elkins. That friend passed it on to someone who didn't know any of the principals, but did know a friend of Wiss. Since then, a few more messages had arrived via the same route, every one of them the same: What's taking so long? Do we have a deal or not? The prosecutors are on our asses.

Wiss and Elkins were making the same reply every time: We're doing it, this is complicated, we'll get you the money before your lawyers run out of stall time. They could only hope this answer would keep Corbett and Dolan satisfied.

And they certainly didn't expect the next message would be delivered in person.

This suburban Elkins played in a softball league, neighborhood teams or company teams, most of the players middle-aged like himself, a few young guys among them. Elkins was in better physical condition than all but a few of the kids in the league, but in softball you didn't need to be in great condition. The ball never moved very fast, and neither did most of the players.

Elkins was one of the heavy bats in the league, so he played right field, except when they were short a player and he played center-right. Today they were playing on a bare field beside a Roman Catholic church with a Polish saint's name, Elkins' neighborhood team versus a team from Baseline Tools. It was an overcast day, a nasty wind whipping across the field out of Canada and across Lake Michigan. Elkins hopped from foot to foot when he was out on the field, trying to keep warm, waiting for the game to end. Finally, in the seventh and last inning, he just managed to race in and catch a looping Texas Leaguer over the second baseman's head, to retire the side and end the game with Elkins' team, the Bearcats, winning three to two.

As he trotted in toward the benches, carrying the ball—which they'd have to use next time—he was surprised to see Wiss among the very few attendees seated on the windy bleacher along the third base line. Wiss didn't normally come watch Elkins play ball, any more than Elkins spent time in Wiss's darkroom. But then Elkins' surprise turned to something else, making him lose the rhythm of his stride, jog with a gimp in it before he got his balance back. Seated next to Wiss on the bleacher was Bob Dolan.

As the teams gathered around home plate, congratulating one another, reminding themselves about the next game in the series, Wiss and Dolan got to their feet and joined the people walking toward the small gravel parking area between the ball field and the church.

Elkins had to spend the next few minutes with his teammates, talking and listening, doing the postmortems, savoring the victory, but his attention was with those two, as they walked away and got into Wiss's car, an anonymous pale green Ford Taurus. The few other cars drove away, out to the street past the church, but the Taurus sat there, pointed at third base.

What was Dolan doing here? The cops were keeping a tight eye on Dolan and Corbett. The law had only agreed to bail in hopes they'd be led to the heisters who'd gotten away, and now Dolan *had* led them here, unless he'd made damn sure he wasn't followed.

But even if he was careful enough, why let the law know he'd taken time out from their radar loop? Elkins, smiling and laughing with his teammates, kept looking past the ball field at the church, the street out front, the looming red brick elementary school some distance the other way. Would those spaces suddenly fill up with blue uniforms? What had Dolan done here? And why?

As soon as he could, Elkins left the ball field, walking around the backstop and over to where he'd left his own car parked at the curb near the church. His vehicle was also deliberately forgettable, a gray Chevy Celebrity. He started the engine, rolled the passenger window partway down, and waited until the green Taurus went by; then he swung in behind it.

Wiss drove them twenty minutes east, across the line into Chicago, before pulling in at the outsized parking lot of a discount hardware store. Elkins, hanging back along the way as much as he could, kept an eye on the rest of the traffic as they went along, and it didn't seem to him that anybody besides himself was interested in following Wiss. Or Dolan.

When neither man got out of the Taurus, Elkins finally left the Celebrity, walked around the intervening parked cars, and slid into the Taurus backseat. "Hello, Bob," he said, trying to be as neutral as possible.

Wiss's worried eyes met Elkins' in the rearview mirror. "Bob's unhappy," he said.

"You don't look happy yourself," Elkins told him. "And fuck knows *I'm* not happy." Leaning forward, forearms on the seatback so he could be close to Dolan, who was half-turned in his seat, mulishly glowering at both of them, he said, "And from the look of you, Bob, you are a long way from happy."

"I'm not a long way from jail, Frank," Dolan said. A bulky-shouldered guy in his late thirties, he had a shelf of bone across his eyebrows that made him look teed off even when he was cheerful. At the moment, quietly, he was teed off. He said, "We're not getting off the dime here."

"*You're* off the dime," Elkins told him. "You're off the reservation, Bob. What's the law think about that?"

"They think I'm quarantined, sick in bed with mumps," Dolan said. "I got a doctor I helped before, he's helping me now. I went out in his coat and hat and drove away in his car, and he's watching TV in my sickbed. Soon another doctor visit, and there I am, never left home."

"I admire that," Elkins said, "but it's still a hell of a chance."

"One I had to take," Dolan said. "Because the prosecutors are going to the judge. This thing's dragging out, they want it off their desk."

"We're getting it done, Bob," Elkins assured him. "You know how tricky that damn place is."

Wiss said, "I've been telling him that."

"Tell the prosecutors," Dolan said. "Except, I don't *think* so. Sometime next week, the judge's gonna hand down a revised order. Either he revokes bail, and Harry and me go inside, or he puts a tracker bracelet on us. Either way, we can't go black any more. Either way, we got no choice, your ears are gonna start burning."

"Next week." Elkins had just heard from Larry Lloyd that Parker said he was almost done dealing with the problems Larry'd fucked up and brought him. Elkins and Wiss were planning to head for Montana tomorrow, and Parker should be there anytime after that.

Except, what did "anytime" mean? What if Parker got held up another week, two weeks? If Dolan and Corbett had this problem, where they could no longer skip out if they were in jail or braceletted, then Elkins and Wiss had a worse problem. They didn't have to be locked up or fitted with a tracker device. They were family men, community men. They couldn't suddenly turn into Jesse James, they wouldn't last a week.

All they could do was hope the lawyers would hold out long enough, and that Parker could deal with his problem quick. Elkins said, "Next week. You make it

Monday, we're probably in trouble. You make it Friday, we're probably okay. That's all I can say."

"Well, you oughta know about it," Dolan said. "Harry and me don't want you guys to take a fall, but we gotta give you warning here. Just in case things don't work out, we don't care if they all of a sudden can't find you. If we sing, we sing, and if you've already lammed, tough shit." Dolan shrugged. "You see what I mean? If *we* can't powder, you two can."

"Thanks for the option, Bob," Elkins said.

Next morning, they took turns driving the Taurus toward Montana. Midway across Minnesota on Interstate 94, with Elkins at the wheel, Wiss said, "I don't usually talk this way, but it might be, things don't go the way we like out here, Bob and Harry would be better off dead."

"They already thought of that, Ralph," Elkins said. "They thought of it before you did."

"Well, I thought of it now," Wiss said.

4

Paul Brock led a charmed life and he knew it. More than once he'd survived when he shouldn't have survived; when Pam Saugherty had saved him instead of jailing him, for instance. More than once he'd fallen in shit and come out smelling like . . . not roses. Like money.

It was unsettling to realize it was the money that had made it possible for him to fall into the shit all over again, this time with maybe no coming out at all. It was the money that had made it possible to spend all this time planning revenge against Parker, to at last find Parker, and to hire somebody to do him down once and for all.

Well, *that* hadn't worked. Not only did Charov turn out not to be the platinum pro he was cracked up to be, not only did Brock make the mistake of turning Parker's attention toward himself, but now his Outfit friends at Cosmopolitan weren't his friends any more. The schmuck who stayed out in the cold, that was Paul Brock.

The truth was, his own revenge jones toward Parker had shrunk away to nothing years ago. It was only for Matt's sake that he'd kept on, only for Matt's sake that he'd exulted when at last Parker's name had popped up on his own Web search, only for Matt's sake that he'd paid Charov the money and got himself into this mess.

What it was, he'd had some vague feeling—not a belief, barely articulated at all—that if he could bring down Parker, if he could *show Matt* that he'd brought down Parker, it would change Matt into something better, much closer to the man he'd used to be. The only man Brock had ever really wanted.

Matt wasn't a man anybody could want, not now. Swollen, bitter, helpless. In the old days, he'd been strong, purposeful, quick. He'd been mean then, too, and brutal, and seemed to take an angry pleasure in hurting women—like Pam—for making him want them. Brock hadn't cared about the meanness back then, because he'd had all the rest of Matt as well. But now the meanness was all.

Brock knew, of course, that killing Parker wouldn't bring back Matt's legs, but in his dream it would bring back Matt's spirit. Instead of which, it had brought the threat of Parker right into their home.

Brock made his living these days mostly by stealing technology for the mob. He owned a computer shop that made a small profit, he did debugging and other technical things for Cosmopolitan and others, but mostly he was the mob guys' computer genius, the one that could get them into closed files, find them everything from insider stock market knowledge to FBI surveillance tapes. They paid him well, or they had until now, when, because of Parker, all at once they'd cut him off. So that was the reason to finish Parker himself, if he could. Not for revenge, not any more, but just to get his livelihood back.

The first thing to do was move Pam out of the house until it was over. Matt hated Pam, and she despised him back. Usually Brock ignored that, because Pam made the household work, and had saved Matt's life, and saved Brock from going to jail. But now, having to watch and wait for Parker, Brock couldn't afford to be distracted. Matt had to stay, there was no choice about that, no chance for the two of them to go somewhere and hide, but Pam had to go.

"Go somewhere south," he told her. "Go somewhere sunny, phone me when you get there, tell me how to get in touch, I'll call you when things are normal here."

She said, "What's going to happen, Paul?" She was worried for him, he knew, not for herself, and certainly not for Matt.

He said, "The man who shot Matt and me, that you saw out front, he's going to try to finish what he started. I'm going to try to stop him. If I do, I'll call you. If I don't . . ." He shrugged, not wanting to think about that alternative.

She patted his arm. "I know you'll be all right," she said.

Neither of them mentioned Matt.

The first thing to do was switch off the circuit breaker to the riding chair that Matt almost never used these days, that made it theoretically possible for him to travel down the one flight of stairs to the other wheelchair, motorized and kept near the front door. Matt was rebellious now, since the threat of Parker had become real, rebellious and angry and unpredictable and probably afraid. Brock didn't want him to suddenly take it into his head to leave the building, go haring off in search of a gun, in search of old friends to help him, in search of the simple relief of movement.

The strange thing, the sad thing, was Brock's realization there *were* no old friends. Matt had always been too rough to have friendships, and the people he'd known had dropped away the instant he was hurt. Brock had many friends, bar friends and techie friends and music friends from his days running a record shop, but now he realized just how shallow those friendships really were. There was no one to stand beside him now. He was on his own.

The next thing was to think about how Parker could get into the building. There was the front door. The rest of the ground floor was a tourist shop, T-shirts and postcards and such, with its own separate entrance, and its own furnace in its own closed-off section of the basement, so there was no access from there. Behind the house, the narrow slate-surfaced space was a closed areaway between this row of brick houses and the larger newer apartment house that faced on the next street.

There was the roof. Most of this block was nineteenth-century row houses, built all together, with the same flat roof. Originally they'd all been single-family residences, like Brock's, but some of the houses were now split up into apartments, with public stairwells. Parker could get into any of those buildings with no problem, make his way to the roof, walk from there over to this roof, and come down through the trapdoor at the top of the stairwell.

When Brock had bought the house, there had been a fire escape down the front of it, but he'd gotten approval from the Landmarks Commission and had it removed. So that meant there were only the two possibilities: the front door and the roof.

Before she'd left, Pam had stocked the place with non-perishable food. There was no reason for Brock to leave the house for the next few days, so no reason to keep that front door functional. He kept a few tools in a kitchen drawer, including a hammer. In the cluttered basement, he found a three-foot length of two-by-four, and an old coffee can that held a mix of screws and nails and drill bits and Allen wrenches. Carrying these upstairs, he nailed the two-by-four to the floor against the inner front door, which opened inward. It wouldn't open now. Let Parker have the small vestibule out there; he wouldn't get through this door.

The trapdoor was more difficult. The way it worked, there was a square hole in the roof, two and a half feet across, with a thick six-inch-high rim on all four sides. A square heavy cover fit over that, not hinged. The way you got out to the roof was to lift the cover straight up, slide it leftward, and set it on the roof.

The sides of the cover came down outside the rim. Two hasp locks opposite each other hung down from the cover just inside the rim, to hook over swivel eyes screwed to the rim. The cover itself was thick wood sheathed in a layer of roofing material, to keep it waterproof.

For the normal run of burglar, the hasps were deterrent enough, giving no sign of weakness to an exploratory tug. But Parker would be more determined, and Brock had known for a long time that the hundred-and-fifty-year-old wood of the rim, as old as the house, had become soft with time, and the screws set into it to hold the swivel eyes were short, to be within the thickness of the rim. A tenacious man with a crowbar could eventually drag those screws out of there, and the lid would lift right off.

He stood at the top landing of the house, next to his bedroom, for a long while, looking up at the trapdoor, one hand holding a rung of the iron ladder bolted to the wall here. Finally, he went back down to the kitchen tool drawer, found the tape measure, carried it upstairs, climbed the ladder, and measured the distance between the hasps, just above the swivels. Twenty-eight and a half inches. He went back down to the kitchen, got out the small saw, and sacrificed a broom, holding it braced above the sink as he cut off the handle at twenty-nine inches. He carried that and the hammer upstairs, and wedged the stick into position, pressed tight against both hasps. Now, upward pressure wouldn't cause the screws to move sideways out of the wood.

Later, he went downstairs and made a simple and not very good dinner for himself and Matt. There was almost no conversation between them at the table, except when Matt said, "What are you doing about it?"

"I've blocked things so he can't get in," Brock told him.

Matt didn't like that. "For how long? A year? Ten years? The thing to do is *let* him in! *Bring* him in, get rid of him for good!"

"We can't do that, Matt."

"*You* can't do it, you fucking faggot! Give me a gun! Let me defend myself against the bastard!"

"I'm keeping him out," Brock said, and wouldn't talk about it any more.

He couldn't sleep. He lay in the dark in his bedroom on the top floor, two stories up from Matt, with faint illumination from the city outside painting the room a dark pinkish gray. His room was at the back, to keep away from street noise, so it was usually quiet up here. It was quiet tonight, but he couldn't sleep.

He was still awake at 2:37 in the morning, by the bedside clock, when he heard the footsteps on the roof. Moving, then stopping. Moving again, stopping again. Silent a long time, as Brock stared at the ceiling, listening to his own heart. Then moving again, moving away.

He's here, Brock thought.

5

If Bert Hayes hadn't instinctively and immediately taken such a strong dislike to Paxton Marino, he probably wouldn't have dug any deeper into the failed Montana burglary, probably would have just taken it at face value. But Hayes couldn't help it, Marino made him wince like a fingernail scraping along a blackboard.

The solid gold toilets themselves, objects of the thieves' intentions, would have been enough to turn Bert Hayes off, but they were nothing compared to the personality of Paxton Marino himself. A jumped-up johnny-come-lately, Marino acted with such smug arrogance it made Hayes want to punch him in the mouth. Marino strolled through life with the self-satisfaction of someone who comes from a long line of rulers of the universe, and goddamn it, he did *not*!

Bert Hayes, a sandy-haired short pugnacious man of forty-three, came from a long line of detectives. His fa-

ther and uncle and great-uncle had all been with the
New York Police Department, and all had made plainclothes. Hayes himself had started with the NYPD, but
his first wife, Marie, had been a high school art
teacher when there was still such a thing, and he'd unexpectedly found in himself a great passion for the
plastic arts. Not as a painter or a sculptor, but as an ap-
preciator and student.

Around the time the marriage with Marie was being
called for lack of interest, Hayes had heard of a job
opening for an art cop at the federal level. He'd ap-
plied, ready for a change of scene, and had been on
that job ever since; nine years now, and counting. He
was with the Art Identification Bureau, a minor under-
funded subset of the Secret Service, which was itself an
element of Alcohol, Tobacco and Firearms, and the mis-
sion of the bureau primarily was to identify stolen artworks imported into the United States. A lot of the
bureau's time and effort went into Holocaust-related
work, trying to connect orphaned art with the descen-
dants of its former owners. More than half a century
later, and Hitler's mess was still being cleaned up.

The Holocaust wasn't all of it, though. A lot of European art was very haphazardly protected from
theft—in many Italian churches, for instance, and in
private country estates in Great Britain—so Old Masters did crop up from time to time, strayed several
thousand miles from home. That's why Hayes was
given a heads-up any time the work of some Old Mas-
ter appeared in conjunction with any kind of crime.

Like the burglary at Paxton Marino's hunting lodge, for instance. An early report, from the local police, had listed among the valuables that had attracted the thieves but had not been spirited away a Rembrandt and a Titian, without titles or descriptions.

That caught Hayes's attention. Usually, he would just glance at such a report and move on to the next, but this time, surprised that such works should be in such a remote setting, he asked for a follow-up, and his curiosity was doubled when the follow-up left the paintings off the list.

Trying to work out what was going on, Hayes started making phone calls, but couldn't get a satisfactory answer from anybody in Montana. Finally, at a time when work had brought him to Los Angeles anyway, he stopped in to see Marino in his little hilltop palace in Bel Air, where the man was so patronizing that Hayes's jaw ached for three days afterward, from clenching his teeth.

And certainly not, Marino had said, there were no *paintings* at his hunting lodge in Montana. Why on earth would he have a *Rembrandt* in *Montana*? Was this an example of government detail work at its best?

Brooding on his Marino encounter afterward, Hayes eventually came to the conclusion that the man was up to something. There was no real reason to believe he was up to something, except for the inconsistency between the two reports, but Hayes had himself convinced of it. So the question was, what was Marino up to, and what could Hayes do about it?

He had no justification to take time off to go to Montana, and wouldn't have known what to do when he got there, but he could make phone calls, and after a while he got to be phone pals with a state CID inspector named Moxon who'd had his own single meeting with Marino, which had been enough to make him loathe the man for life. Moxon agreed to keep an eye on Marino's lodge, and let Hayes know if anything unusual happened.

And now something had. Moxon phoned to say, "A private plane came up from Texas to Great Falls with a shipment of wooden crates. A fella I know at Customs there told me about it."

Hayes said, "Customs wouldn't have anything to do with it, if it came from Texas."

"No, but it isn't that big an airport, and my friend saw the stuff, and wondered about it. They're big thin padded crates."

Hayes sat up. "Like crates you'd use to ship paintings?"

"Could be, I wouldn't know that sort of thing myself. But here's the two things about them. There's labels on all of them, say they're property of the Horace Griffith gallery in Dallas."

Writing that down, Hayes said, "And the other thing?"

"Well, they're empty," Moxon said. "This Horace Griffith is spending a bunch of money and a private plane to send Paxton Marino a dozen empty crates. Thought you'd like to know."

6

"Released today from the federal minimum-security facility at Broadghent, Brad Grenholz, one-time high-flying Internet innovator . . ."

He's out, Lloyd thought, and frowned at the small screen. Because the terms of his parole included his agreement to stay away from the Net and from computers entirely, the components he'd assembled into this supposed music equipment in his study were all miniaturized, including the screen. He could see the entire picture, very small, or a quarter of the picture at a time. But with most text, by leaning in close and removing his glasses, he could read enough to get the idea. This time, he had the idea all right.

Brad was out. His so-called partner, the man who'd cheated him, the man he'd tried to kill and to steal from, the man who had so unbalanced him that he'd done all those things that had led him straight into prison, that rotten son of a bitch was out.

And he wasn't even supposed to be. He'd been stealing from the *feds,* and was supposed to stay inside another three or four years at the least. But, reading deeper into the news report, Lloyd saw that Brad had become part of a federal housecleaning project, thinning out the population in overcrowded prisons by early release of some non-violent inmates with good career and rehabilitation prospects.

Brad fit that profile because he was going back into business with George Carew, his one-time lawyer and still brother-in-law, who would bring Brad into his new and already successful on-line legal consultancy. George would also take legal responsibility for Brad, and house him until he got back on his feet.

In that case, Lloyd knew where Brad was. With all his new money, some of it stolen from Lloyd, George Carew had built himself a mansion on Cape Ann, east of Ipswich, less than forty miles north of Boston, a gabled and turreted monstrosity on a rocky height overlooking the cape and the Atlantic beyond, something straight out of the Brontë sisters. George had rooms in that place he hadn't even named yet, much less furnished and occupied; there would be plenty of room for Brad there.

And George would take Brad in, help him "until he got back on his feet," because Brad, unlike Lloyd, had kept his mouth shut. The time Brad had done had been for George as well.

I could go there, Lloyd thought. He switched off the machine and left the study and spent the rest of that day and evening thinking how he and Brad were in the same state now, less than three hours apart, and he could go see Brad if he wanted, talk to him if he wanted.

But why would he want to? He had no desire to lose his self-control again, so what point was there in confrontation? He could only show himself to be weak, a loser, a second-rater stuck in the past. Winners move on to the new game.

I'll be a winner, Lloyd told himself. I'll move on to the new game, and this robbery in Montana will make it possible. I won't try to meet with Brad, not now. Not until *I'm* back on my feet.

Unsure he'd be able to sleep, he'd taken a pill when going to bed, so they had to pound on the door quite a while before they roused him, which made them even more impatient and angry, pushing him around for no reason at all. Half a dozen state cops, four in uniform and two in plainclothes, questioning him about anything and everything in his life, demanding to make a complete search of the entire house, an intrusion much more serious and difficult than anything they'd ever done to him before.

He was so groggy from the pill that they'd been there almost an hour, prying, prodding, making a mess in every room they searched, before he realized what this had to be. It was because Brad had been released. They were telling him, stay away from your old partner, stay away from the guy you tried to kill. They never mentioned Brad's name, and neither did Lloyd, but that was what it was all about.

Thank God he hadn't kept the gun. When Parker had made him clean up, after he'd been so stupid as to shoot that man in the face, he'd thought at first he might keep the gun, hide it somewhere, but then decided he wasn't somebody who should trust himself with a gun. So he'd stuffed it inside the tarp that held the body, and gun and body went together over that bridge into the river. Right now he was very relieved he'd made that choice, because this search of the house was *thorough*. They would have found the gun. And then he would *never* have been out of jail again, his entire life.

But they didn't find the computer, the Web access. They never did, and they never would, because he'd made it look so convincingly like something else. He had that tiny victory, at least.

What they did accomplish, though, that they'd never accomplished before, was at last to break his confidence that he would ever someday climb out of this mess. When he asked one of the plainclothesmen, near the end, "Why are you doing this?" the man smirked at him, and said, "Because we can."

"That's no *reason*."

"We don't need a reason," the plainclothesman told him. "You're our hobby, Lloyd, and we'll come around and play anytime we want."

The pill had worn off by the time they left, at four in the morning. The pill had worn off, and so had his belief that he could go on being Larry Lloyd, that somewhere down the line he would return to the life and the self that had once been his. They weren't going to let him. They were never going to let him.

4:12 A.M., the computer told him, when he clicked it on. He went directly into the American Airlines computer, as he'd done more than once before, and made it give him a first-class ticket on tomorrow afternoon's flight from Boston's Logan Airport to Lambert in St. Louis, in the name of Larry Perkins. Months ago, he'd persuaded the Department of Motor Vehicles computer in Boston to give him a driver's license in that name, which he would show at the ticket counter at Logan tomorrow.

4:27 A.M., the computer told him, when he shut it down, disassembled it, trashed it so that no one would ever know what it had been or what it had known and done. Quickly he moved through the house, taking only what he felt he absolutely needed. He had a lot to do, and very little time to do it in.

5:03 read the dashboard clock on his old Honda Accord when he started it up and drove out of his house for the last time.

11:00 A.M. Lloyd remembered George Carew's house, remembered being shown around it, remembered visiting three or four times back when they were all still supposedly friends.

The place was set near the apex of a high triangle of land that jutted eastward out over Cape Ann. An electric fence stretched across the base of the triangle, a quarter mile east of the nearest coastal road. George owned all the land from road to cliff, but had only cleared the triangle, leaving the pine-and-laurel woods intact over the rest of the property, with a narrow gravel access road through it.

There was no way to get through from the front unobserved and unobstructed. That left the approach from the sea.

There was no real beach in that area, merely a sloping rock face covered with stones and pebbles that rose up from the water to meet the boulder-and-dirt cliff face. The cliff wasn't vertical, but steep, with irregular setbacks. Scrub trees clutched to the steep slope, sometimes blown away in ocean storms. George had planned to give himself ocean access with a series of staircases down from the house, but Lloyd doubted he'd done it. George's relationship with nature was as observer, through a window, not as participant, running up and down outside staircases.

A mile farther north of George's property, a seafood restaurant had been built, where the land was much nearer sea level and the coastal road had swung in close to the cape. Lloyd left the Honda in the parking lot there and walked south along the shoreline, over the rough shifting surface of loose pebbles. It was hard going, but the tide was mostly out, so he had a wide enough swath of fairly level ground to make his way along.

When he reached George's triangle, the house was invisible from below, but he knew where it was. And no, as he'd expected, the staircases had not been built.

Lloyd wasn't a very physical type himself, but he could do it when he had to. He looked to see where the slope was least steep, with the most setbacks, and with enough trees to hold on to on the way up, and started to climb.

It was about sixty feet up, about as tall as a six-story building, but the climb was much steeper than any staircase. Several times he had to pull himself upward, clinging with both hands to the rough hard trunk of a scraggy pine, and three times he had to pause at a relatively flat spot to sit awhile, pant, wait for the trembling in his arms and legs to ease.

But at last he was there. He straightened, holding to two shrubs, and could just look over the lip of the land across manicured lawn to the hulking dark stone house. No one was in sight.

The top few feet were the steepest, and the lawn itself had no handholds for him, so at first he couldn't make the transition, and looking down from here was making him dizzy. Heart pounding, he crab-sidled to the right until he found a place where jutting teeth of stone and the grayed stumps of two small trees cut away by George's gardener to improve the view gave him footholds so he could crawl up and over the edge,

chest on the stubbly November grass as he pulled himself along by his elbows.

He didn't stand. The house was about twenty feet
away, its many windows glittering in the late-morning
sun. For anybody in the house, that sun would make it
harder to see outside right now, but if he were to stand
up he'd still be very noticeable.

On all fours, he crawled over to the house, stood at
last against its rough stone, and moved around it to
the left. As he remembered it, the kitchens—there
were two—were around on this side, with the delivery
entrance.

Yes. The doors here were all massive and dark, new
made to look old, imported from Scotland. With
strong security across the front of the property, and
the cliff and ocean at the rear, there was no reason to
lock any of the doors here by day, so Lloyd just opened
this one and walked in.

The first kitchen he came to was empty. There was
a small bathroom off it, and he realized his nervous-
ness had made it necessary for him to use it. While in
there, he studied himself in the mirror and saw he was
a mess, hands and face scratched from the climb,
clothing rumpled and dirty, hair turned into a fright
wig. He washed, patted down his clothing, made himself look as neat as he could, then stepped outside to
find a maid now in the kitchen. Before he could decide what to do, she nodded at him, murmured something in Spanish, and went on with her work.

So luck was with him. If he'd still looked the same

mess as a few minutes ago, she wouldn't have mistaken him for a houseguest. Smiling at her, feeling all at once less nervous, he strode confidently from the kitchen.

For the next twenty minutes, he roamed the house. From time to time he saw or heard people, heard George's voice from a nearby room once, saw servants, saw people who were not servants but whom he didn't know, but he made certain no one after that first maid saw him. He was ready with lies and evasions if he did unexpectedly bump into somebody, but it didn't happen.

He roamed the downstairs, saw lunch being prepared, then took the grand major staircase, which split at the top to go left and right, both sides coming to the same large second-floor hall. There were mostly bedrooms and baths along here, and in the third bedroom on the left, when he opened the door, there was Brad, seated on an unmade bed, wearing a green polo shirt and tan chinos and pulling on a black sock. He looked up with surprise, and if that was actually fear Lloyd saw on his face for just an instant, it was immediately gone, as Brad leaped up from the bed with that false booming good fellowship Lloyd remembered so well, one sock on, one foot bare, spreading his arms as he cried, "Larry! My God, look at you!"

And all at once, Lloyd was himself again. The nerd, the follower, the number two, the fellow born to be a sidekick. The years on his own had, after all, been horrible ones, left to make his own decisions, with no one to trail after and obey. Brad was a leader, and needed Larry. Larry was a follower, and needed Brad. It was as simple as that.

Lloyd stood there, stunned at himself more than at Brad, and accepted the bear hug Brad gave him, without actually responding. Then Brad stepped back, looked him up and down, grinning like any college pal in the presence of his old college pal once more, saying, "Let me look at you. You've changed."

"We both have."

It was true. Time and prison had hardened them both, though it was less obvious in Brad. He'd always been sure of himself, and seemed now like a man it would actually be dangerous to cross.

And I thought, Lloyd told himself, I thought *I* was going to be dangerous to cross. What a fool I am.

Brad said, "How did you do this? What a surprise! Why didn't you phone? I guess you saw the ink I got."

"Yes, I read it," Lloyd said. "Non-violent. Ready to be rehabilitated."

"That's me," Brad said, and laughed. "You gonna come back with me, Larry? We'll kick the shit out of them, you and me."

Lloyd was bewildered by the both of them. Shouldn't Brad be full of recriminations, because Lloyd had ratted him out? Shouldn't Lloyd be full of recriminations, because Brad had stolen from him and humiliated him? But somehow they seemed to have gone immediately past all that, to be already at a new relationship. Or the old relationship, as though nothing had ever happened.

But things *had* happened. Looking around, trying to get his bearings, Lloyd saw, on the antique dresser, a bottle of red wine, half drunk, the cork stuck back in it. He said, "Still taking the wine to bed with you?"

"It's been years since I could, baby," Brad said. "But *you* know about that, you've been there. Listen, what happened to your face? You've got scratches there."

Walking to the dresser, Lloyd said, "I came up the cliff. Okay if I look at this?"

"Sure," Brad said, as Lloyd picked up the bottle and read the label. "You came up the *cliff*?"

"Uh-huh."

"For God's sake, why?"

"Well," Lloyd said, "I came to kill you." And he swung the bottle as hard as he could into that smiling lying face.

Brad staggered back, hands coming up toward his face, and Lloyd pursued him, swinging the bottle again, just as hard.

The third time, the bottle smashed, leaving him with the jagged neck. After that, it got easier.

Larry Perkins made his St. Louis flight out of Logan with half an hour to spare.

7

It was turning out to be one of those days. Dave Rappleyea didn't like it when it turned out to be one of those days, and fortunately, here at the lodge, those days were infrequent. But this was turning out to be one of them.

By "one of those days," Dave Rappleyea meant a day with incidents in it. A good day, as far as he was concerned, had no incidents in it at all. A good day was one where he could sit quietly at his station in front of the bank of security monitors and play DoomRangers II from the beginning of his tour at eight A.M. through lunch at noon brought to him at the station by Myrna or Fred, till the end of his tour at four. A good day was also one in which the roster had not yet rotated back to him being the one to go up to the main house after dinner to flush all the toilets and walk through all the rooms so the sensors and monitors could make note of him, and the duty guy would therefore know that everything at the main house was still working the way it was supposed to.

Of the eight resident staff members here at Paxton Marino's hunting lodge in Montana, five of them, one of the women and four of the men, were simple obsessive geeks, happy with their own company and their own pastime, like Dave. For instance, one was an amateur naturalist, spending all his free time out in the woods, turning over rocks, collecting slugs and ants and all kinds of wriggly crap, while another one was Net crazy, lurking in chat rooms all her waking hours, adding her address to more and more monster mailing lists, receiving endless dumb jokes or chain letters through the ether and dutifully passing them on.

The remaining three staff, one woman and two men, were silent anti-social secret-hoarders, people who would have joined the French Foreign Legion if they spoke the language. Warily they guarded their personal stories from everybody else, none of whom cared. And none of them were aware that, in hiring them, Marino's personnel people had been following the guidelines they'd been given for this low-level job in this isolated place; self-sufficient compulsives who wouldn't get bored and, even more important, wouldn't get curious.

It was pretty much a democracy the staff had worked out here, developing their systems from scratch, none of them having known any of the others before they'd been hired on here. All had backgrounds in security and knew the role without having to be overseen. Greg was technically the boss, who could give them orders if he wanted to, but Greg was one of the paranoid three, and preferred no contact with other human beings at all.

So it was usually a good gig, this little house halfway up the mountain, an anti-community of solitaries. Dave Rappleyea had never been so content in his life. Except, of course, every once in a while, when there was one of *those* days.

This one had begun with a phone call, which Dave had logged in at 9:38 A.M. It was the duty man's (or woman's) job to deal with any incoming from the outer world, as well as to monitor security up at the main house, so when the phone rang, it was Dave's job to punch the outside-line button on the console in front of himself (very like a *Star Trek* control room), pick up the receiver, and say, "Lodge," the sufficiently minimal approved response on the phone that wouldn't give too much away.

"Oh, ello."

The call was from a snobby English-sounding woman who said she was calling from Texas, that she was the executive assistant of Horace Griffith, and that Mr. Griffith would be arriving at Great Falls airport at one this afternoon and would require to be met.

Dave knew who Horace Griffith was. A very fancy-schmancy art dealer that Mr. Marino bought pictures from, some of them on walls here at the lodge, over fireplaces or sofas, all of them European and old, all of them dull as anything, none of them as visually exciting as even one frame of DoomRangers II. Whenever Mr. Griffith came to the lodge, there was a certain amount of extra activity, but not normally too irritatingly distracting.

Dave agreed he'd have someone drive down to meet Mr. Griffith—that would be Fred, today—and the woman said there would also be a shipment coming up with Mr. Griffith, in a hired truck with a hired driver. "Mr. Marino has approved," she assured him.

Mr. Marino *had* to approve, that was the rule, he had to approve every single person who entered the property, and that went double these days, ever since that insane robbery attempt a couple months ago. These days, security at the lodge was tighter than ever, including those weird lights on all night, and added motion sensors, and all the rest of it.

And tightened procedures, as well. Being as diplomatic as possible, Dave said to the woman, "I guess Mr. Griffith will be bringing written approval from Mr. Marino with him. I mean for the truck."

The woman sighed, elaborately. "Is that really necessary?" She pronounced it *ness*-iss-ry.

"If I want to keep my job, ma'am, yes, it is."

That of course made it different; they were both employees, after all. "I'll arrange to have Mr. Marino fax the approval," she promised, and forty-five minutes later it did come clicking in.

It was legitimate, all right. It was on one of Mr. Marino's letterheads, it was signed with his usual

cramped little up-and-down signature, and it had been
sent from his fax number in Courmayeur:

> Mr. Horace Griffith will be arriving today to
> spend one night, possibly two, at the lodge. Give
> him every assistance. He will be bringing with
> him a number of wooden crates, to be trans-
> ported to the lodge in a vehicle rented from Big
> Sky Motor Transport. The crates will be un-
> loaded at the lodge by staff, and the truck will de-
> part. At a later time, to be determined by Mr.
> Griffith, the truck will return, and Mr. Griffith
> will oversee the loading of a second shipment of
> crates, to be taken away from the lodge.

Well, that was straightforward, and didn't seem as
though it should create too much of a ripple in the
otherwise placid circle of days at the lodge.

That's what Dave thought. At eleven-thirty, Fred left
to pick up Mr. Griffith, Dave watching the white Blazer
on the monitors as it swerved down the twisty road off
the mountain, and it was still more or less a normal
day. And it still was at quarter to three, when Fred ra-
dioed Dave from the Blazer: "ETA in five minutes,
we'll go straight up to the lodge."

"Roger."

Dave intercommed this info to Greg, then watched
Greg and Bob and Wilma move from camera to camera through the house, then outside to climb into another of the Blazers and drive on up to the lodge.

And here came Blazer number one, back up the road, this time followed by a big boxy truck with a black cab but the body painted a bright pale blue; the big sky, maybe. Dave looked away from DoomRanger II, his thumbs still on the controls, to watch those vehicles come up, bypass the house, and head on up to the lodge.

Up there, Greg and Bob and Wilma stood by the open front door, and here came the other two vehicles. Fred and Mr. Griffith, a trim middle-aged man with a haughty manner and a thick crown of wavy white hair, got out of their car as the truck made a cumbersome U-turn to put its rear as close as possible to the front door.

Two men in work clothes got out of the truck, as Wilma collected Mr. Griffith's suitcase from the Blazer and carried it into the lodge.

The next few minutes were just people carrying things; no reason for Dave to look up from his battle. Wilma took Mr. Griffith's suitcase to his guest room, while the two men from the truck carried crate after crate into the front hall, each crate a large narrow rectangle, the smallest four feet square, the largest five by eight.

Inside, following Mr. Griffith, Greg and Bob and Fred, and after her other errand Wilma, carried the crates to the basement door and downstairs, the only place in the whole compound that wasn't covered by the monitor cameras. Dave supposed that was because, if any unauthorized person had gotten that far, they would already have been seen by half a dozen cameras elsewhere, so what difference would it make to see the same person in the basement? Not that it mattered to him.

His interest now was mostly in DoomRanger II, but his eye was naturally caught by movements on the screens, so he did remain aware of the steady routine of transferring crates from truck to basement, and then all at once his eye was drawn to a different screen, and he saw a different kind of motion.

A bus. Black or dark blue, coming up the road from the state highway. No, that was second, behind a black car. A car and bus coming up the road.

Dave was about to reach for his microphone, to alert Greg up at the lodge that they had interlopers, when his eye was snagged again, this time by *another* kind of movement, on four different screens, showing the steep wooded slope above the lodge.

Men. Men all in black, carrying guns, rifles, walking down the road there, and down through the woods. Men in bulky dark vinyl coats.

The car and bus approached the house from the south. The men in black approached the lodge from the north. It *was* DoomRanger II! But it couldn't be. Then what was it?

There were white letters on the backs of the black vinyl coats of the invaders coming down from the north. One of them passed close enough to a camera, moving away, on down the hill, so the letters could be read on his back: ATF.

ATF? Dave knew what that was, that was Alcohol, Tobacco and Firearms, one of the government police
forces, like the FBI. Somebody'd had a joke about
them a few years ago, Dave remembered: "Alcohol, tobacco, and firearms? Sounds like a party to *me.*"

But this wasn't a party. What the heck was this?
What was the ATF doing *here*? What could they possibly think was going on here?

Trembling, dropping DoomRanger II into his lap,
Dave reached for the mike, thumbed the button, qua-
vered, "Greg! We got— We got—" He stumbled, bewildered between saying *we got visitors* and *we got
company.* "Greg! We got Alcohol, Tobacco and
Firearms!"

And that's when it turned into one of those days;
big time.

8

Matt knew he was coming. The son of a bitch was going to get through Paul's stupid defenses, he'd go through Paul like a saber through a baby, and here was Matt, stuck, in this useless body, in this miserable *wheelchair*!

Paul had shut off the stairclimber. He'd run it on down to the ground floor, by that door he'd nailed shut—as though *that* would do any good—and then he'd cut off the power, so that Matt couldn't use it, couldn't *move*, couldn't get *out* of here, couldn't *defend* himself!

He hated this body. He remembered who he used to be, when he was someone who wasn't afraid of anybody, when he was stronger than anybody and more reckless than anybody and tougher than anybody, so if anybody ever had reason to be afraid, it was the people who had to deal with Matt Rosenstein.

If only he had a gun. He was trapped in these rooms, the kitchen at the front, the living-dining room in the middle, his room at the back. He had windows to look out of, front and back. He had staircases up and down, which he couldn't use. He had knives, in the kitchen, but what good were knives if you couldn't *reach* the guy?

He had telephones, kitchen and bedroom, but they were merely little metal mockeries, jeering him. Who would he call? Who *could* he call? After the trail he'd cut through people, the first part of his life, who was there in the world for him to phone right now, and what would he say? "Hi, this is Matt Rosenstein, you remember me, I broke your jaw one time, I'm stuck here paralyzed in this wheelchair with a guy coming to kill me, I was wondering if you'd like to come help me out."

His arms were still strong, and his brain still worked, you could be sure of that. He had taken a cleaver from the kitchen drawer, not the longest one but the strongest, a solid slice of steel with a firm black handle, shaped for his fist. It was concealed now in the wheelchair against his left hip, blade down, handle toward the front, so he could reach over with the right hand, bring it up and out in one steady motion. If he could get Parker within range . . .

That was the damn thing of it. If he could get his hands on Parker, he had a chance. He might even be able to do him with just the strength in his arms, not even using the knife. But why would Parker get that close?

What could Matt do to bring Parker close? He

thought of lying doggo, pretending to be dead, maybe
with the knife slack in his hand, blood smeared on the
knife and blood smeared on his throat, as though he'd
killed himself. Got in a funk because Parker was coming, and checked out.

Would Parker come over to study the situation up
close, make sure Matt was really dead? Or would he
stand across the room and pump bullets into him from
there, just to be on the safe side? Matt put himself in
Parker's position, gunning down a man in a wheelchair,
finding him maybe dead with a knife in his hand, and
what would Matt do? He knew what he'd do.

Money. Not the knife, the knife concealed at his right
side, held in his right hand, a wad of bills clutched in
his left in his lap, very obvious, as though he'd been
scheming some escape route out of here, somebody to
pay off. A wad of bills, make sure there was at least a
century showing at the top, or better yet a Cleveland, if
they had one here.

They did have stashes of money in the house. Paul
and Matt both came from a life in which it was a good
idea to keep ready cash on tap, just in case. Matt had
money in the well behind a dresser drawer in his room,
but he didn't think there was anything larger than a
hundred there.

Would Paul have a thou? Would he give it or loan it
to Matt? Would that son of a bitch Paul do *anything* to
help Matt out, the bastard?

He could hear Paul walking around, upstairs. Usually, Paul was on the top floor, as far as he could get

from Matt—as though Matt wouldn't have noticed *that*—with Pam Saugherty's room on the floor between. But now Pam was gone, and Paul was afraid of Parker coming down through the roof somehow, so he'd moved down to Pam's room. Changed the sheets, too, Matt had heard that laundering, the machines being up there on Pam's level, and had a good sardonic laugh over it. No, Paul wouldn't like to sleep on sheets smelling of some *woman,* would he? Oh, no, not Paul.

Pam was the last woman Matt had ever had. He realized that all at once, with some surprise, then some regret, regret yet again, in another and equally biting way; all those women he hadn't been able to get his hands on.

Too bad the last one couldn't have been a better article.

Restless, he wheeled around and around his tiny cage, these few rooms, like a lab rat in an experiment, captured and hobbled and placed here in a "natural" environment. Paul had given him canned soup and salted crackers for dinner, and a bottle of beer that had made him giddy for just a few minutes—he couldn't handle booze any more, not at all the way he used to—and then silently Paul had cleaned up the dishes and gone back upstairs, leaving Matt here to wheel himself back and forth, back and forth.

Look out the front windows at the nighttime street, people walking by, to and from their own dinners, cabs going by, sometimes a horn sounding, every once in a while a siren farther off. Look out the back windows at

darkness below, lit windows all around covered by
shades or drapes or blinds.

Would he come from down there, from that lake of
darkness behind the house? Climb up the brick wall
like Spiderman, smash through this window, this window right here. Matt spun the wheelchair wheels, spinning away, rolling forward again, out of the bedroom,
around the dining table, forward to the front windows,
where every lone pedestrian could be Parker.

He'd come late at night, wouldn't he? Matt had
wanted to sleep during the day, but his mind was raging
too much, furious and afraid, and the parts of his body
he could feel ached with tension, across the shoulders
and the back of the neck.

Ten-thirty at night. When would he come, three, four
in the morning? If only Matt could sleep *now*, to be
ready then.

Paul kept moving around upstairs, small mouse-like
rustlings. I need him, Matt thought, and the thought
grated on him, it was like acid. But it was true. He
couldn't get through this on his own.

So at last he wheeled himself to the stairwell, waited
there a minute, red-eyed, glaring at the steps he
couldn't climb, before crying, "Paul!" But it came out
hoarse, not loud enough, a rusty croaking sound. He
didn't speak enough, had nobody to talk to, nothing to
say. He inhaled, burning his throat, and tried again:
"Paul!"

This time Paul heard, up there, and Matt followed
the sound of his hurried footsteps, then saw Paul at the

top of the stairs, gawking downward, his own fear naked on his face. "What is it? Did you hear something?"

"No, I didn't *hear* anything, I didn't *see* anything, I don't *know* anything." He gripped the wheelchair arms, knowing he had to be less hostile, he needed Paul now. "Come down," he said, and paused, and shook his head, and said, "Paul, please come down. We got to talk, we got to work this out."

Paul hesitated. "Do you need your bag changed?"

Hell! That was the most disgusting part of it, the worst part of it, the most degrading part of his helplessness. *"No!"* Then he made fists, and punched his dead thighs, and squeezed his eyes shut. "I want to talk," he said, as calmly as he could, inside the blackness with his eyes shut. "I just want to talk, figure this out. Figure out what to do."

"Oh, sure, Matt, good idea."

Paul came trotting down the stairs, and when Matt opened his eyes he saw that Paul's face was happy now, behind the worry and fear. He'd always used Paul's love, always taken advantage of it, but he'd always hated it, too, recoiled from it the way he now recoiled from his own body. But he still needed Paul. He needed him all the time, for everything in his life, but never more than right now.

He spun away from that open face, not wanting to have to see it, and wheeled into the dining area again, and then forward. He could look out the front windows, that would be all right. Fewer pedestrians now, less traffic.

Paul followed him, but not all the way. He stood back by the dining table, watching him. Matt sensed him back there and blinked out the window, then turned the wheelchair to face Paul. Being very calm, he said, "I figure, he'll come in late, three or four in the morning, probably tonight."

Paul put both hands next to each other on top of a dining table chair, kneaded the wood as though it were dough. "You don't think we can keep him out?"

"He'll get in," Matt insisted. "I think we have to take turns staying awake, one of us on guard. And I think we have to stay together, not separated."

"I suppose you're right." Paul looked around. "I could bring a mattress down," he decided, "just for . . . just for now. Put it right here on the floor."

"When I'm on guard, and you're asleep," Matt said, still being calm, still being reasonable, "you'll have to give me the gun."

Paul blinked at him, but instead of arguing he said, "Matt, I don't have a gun."

"Oh, don't *do* that, Paul!" Matt punched the chair arm. "You can *trust* me, you don't have to be so god-damn *afraid* of me all the time!"

Paul shook his head. "I do have to be afraid of you," he said. "You're too angry. I never know what you might do."

"Do!" Matt spread his arms, to display himself. "What the fuck can I *do*?"

"You can take it out on me," Paul said, and something crashed downstairs.

They both stared. It had been a booming noise, echoing in the stairwell. Something hard had hit the front door.

"It's him!" Paul whispered, turning to stare at the hall, and the something hard smashed into the door again.

Matt knew what that was. It was a ram, the kind of ram the police use to break down a door, a yard-long hollow metal cylinder, closed at both ends, with two handles on top and a conical iron weight inside. Swing it back, pause, and the weight slides to the back of the cylinder. Swing it forward into the door, and the weight comes faster, pounding the end of the cylinder against the door.

This door was nailed, but only at the bottom. The ram would hit it at waist height. The closed vestibule down there would contain most of the noise, and Parker would only swing the ram when no one was outside, walking by. The door wouldn't last long.

A third boom echoed, and Matt wheeled fast at Paul, grabbing his arm with his left hand, clenching him tight before Paul could duck out of the way. "Give me the gun!"

"No! I don't have a—"

"*Give* it to me!" Matt shook him like a dust rag, and Paul's head flopped back and forth, his mouth gabbling, the words all jumbled together. "Give me the gun!"

The crash from downstairs now was a different sound, the sound of the door frame splintering. Matt's right hand flashed down to his left hip, came out with the knife, held it high. "Give me the *gun*, you useless faggot, let *me* take care of the bastard!"

"Hurting— You're hurting—"

The final crash from downstairs, and the volume of the air changed. He's coming up. Matt howled without words, slashing with the knife, over and over, until Paul was a limp thing dangling from the grip of his left hand.

Christ, why didn't you give me the gun? Shit, he's coming up, where is it, where is it?

Matt yanked Paul's body across his lap, frisked it desperately, one-handed, knife in the other as he patted all the pockets, searching, searching . . .

There was no gun. There was no weapon of any kind. How could Paul not have a gun?

Matt looked up, and Parker stood in the doorway. *He* had a gun, a small snub pistol in his right hand. Matt lifted the slippery red knife, but there was no threat in it. He knew he was no threat. He stared at Parker, and Parker stepped forward to look at the scene. Matt let go of Paul's arm, and the body slid off his lap onto the floor. Parker looked at it, at the knife, around at the room, and at last into Matt's eyes. He shook his head. "You aren't worth much," he said, and turned around, and walked away.

9

Ralph Wiss had two sons, but neither of them had followed in his footsteps. Partly that was because they had no idea where his footsteps had taken him, just exactly how he'd made his living all these years, and partly it was because he'd rather they didn't follow the path he'd picked. It had worked out well for him, but not for everybody; a lot of people had found danger and disaster down that road, jail terms or death.

So his own preference was that the boys take up some other profession, if they could find one that pleased them and that they were suited for, and it seemed to be working out. Bobby was in the navy, maybe planning to make a career out of it, and Jason was assistant manager of a supermarket and thinking he might stay with that company over the long haul, all of which was fine.

Still, it did make Wiss feel a little alone now and

then, that he wasn't able to pass on his expertise and experience to a son. Which, in a weird way, was where Larry Lloyd came in. He reminded Wiss a little of himself, the same love of arcane learning, the same ability to concentrate on the smallest details. He was a little too old to be Wiss's son, unless Wiss had started a lot younger than he had, but there was something of that relationship growing there. Not to make a big deal about it, but Larry was in some ways the extra son that Wiss had never had, the son that would continue the family business.

And now Larry was changed, but Wiss thought maybe in a good way. All of a sudden he was there, in Chinook, unexpectedly, loose and grinning, saying, "I don't have to do it long-distance any more."

Wiss and Elkins had taken adjoining motel rooms in Chinook, twenty miles from Havre, and Larry was there waiting for them outside their rooms when they came back from lunch. "I got the next room over," he said.

They went inside, away from a clear cold wind, into Wiss's room, flanked by the rooms of the other two, and Wiss said, "Larry? What about your parole?"

"I decided I'd rather be on the lam," Larry said. "Got tired of playing their game." He was very relaxed, very pleased with himself. Wiss knew it was a stupid comparison, but to him Larry looked like a guy who'd just paid off a heavy mortgage.

Elkins had sensed it, too, but was made worried by it. He said, "Larry, are you hot?"

"Well, sure," Larry said. "I told you, I'm on the lam."

"I mean hotter than that," Elkins said.

Now Larry looked a little uncomfortable, but still pleased with himself, like a kid with a guilty secret. "Frank," he said, "we don't ask each other things like that."

"We do," Elkins told him, "if it can come bite us on the ass. Is the motel manager down there looking at your picture on the TV news right now?"

"Oh, I doubt it," Larry said. "Not way out here."

Now Wiss was sharing Elkins' worry. He said, "Larry, are you on television *anywhere*?"

"Probably," Larry said, shrugging it off, not worried at all. "Around Boston, I suppose."

"Just tell us, Larry," Wiss said. "What did you do?"

Larry ducked his head and spread his hands. "Okay, okay," he said, "you'll hear about it somewhere anyway, doesn't make any difference. You know that ex-partner of mine that I tried to kill."

Wiss said, "You took another crack at him."

"This time I did it right," Larry assured them. "This time, Brad does *not* get rehabilitated."

"Keep a low profile while you're here," Elkins advised him. "We'll bring your meals in to you. After the job, we'll line you up with a plastic surgeon."

"That would be good," Larry agreed. "I can change everything else about myself on the Net, but not my face. But let me go set up my stuff, start listening to those people. We're gonna do the job soon, right?"

"Whenever Parker gets here," Elkins said.

"I can hardly wait."

Larry went off to his own room, and Elkins turned his worried frown toward Wiss, saying, "Just how crazy is he?"

"I'm not sure," Wiss said. He didn't want to admit he was on Larry's side. He said, "I think maybe a little less crazy than before. Maybe he can concentrate better now."

"Just so he concentrates on staying out of sight," Elkins said.

Larry did, for about an hour, and then he knocked on the connecting door between his room and Wiss's. Wiss and Elkins were in there playing gin rummy. Elkins went on looking at the cards while Wiss got up and went over to open the door.

Larry was not grinning now. He said, "Trouble."

Wiss said, "You were seen?"

"Not trouble with *me*," Larry said, coming into the room. "There's a lot of e-mail traffic from the lodge, and phone traffic, and shortwave radio."

Elkins put his cards down. "Shortwave?"

"There's federal cops up there," Larry told him. "I think a lot of them."

Elkins dropped his cards and got to his feet. "What the hell for?"

"They're looking for our paintings," Larry said.

FOUR

1

Parker changed planes at O'Hare, called Wiss from there to pick him up later in Great Falls, and then walked toward his next terminal. Abruptly he stopped, in the pedestrian traffic, to look in at an open-faced snack bar beside the corridor. On a television set behind the bar was a picture of Larry Lloyd.

Parker stepped closer, but he couldn't hear what was being said behind that picture. It was a mug shot, a few years old, head-on to the camera, with the usual look of a mug shot; urgent, but defeated. Then it was replaced by a picture of a burning apartment house.

Farther along the corridor was a newsstand. There was nothing about Lloyd in the *New York Times* or *USA Today,* but an extensive piece in the *Boston Globe.* Parker bought it, and read about Lloyd on the next plane.

It was the emotional thing again. The guy who'd

screwed Lloyd had got an early release, and that tipped him over the edge. But all the way over this time; no more playing computer games, pretending to be here when you're there. There was no way to cover *these* tracks.

What would Lloyd do? Parker didn't think he was the suicidal type, he was too self-righteous for that. He couldn't leave the country, and he had no history as a lamster. There was already a reward posted, from somebody called George Carew, the brother-in-law that Lloyd's enemy and victim had been released to. It was only five thousand so far, but Carew was rich, and would up the ante if he had to, though he probably wouldn't have to.

Where would Lloyd turn? To somebody he'd known on the inside? Almost any one of them would trade him in for five thousand without thinking twice.

What did that mean for the heist? Could they get in without Lloyd running interference on the computer? If they had to just smash in, noisy and direct, that wouldn't be any good, because it would leave them with just the one exit, back down the private road to the state highway. They couldn't repeat Elkins' and Wiss's stunt of going up over the mountain into Canada, because this time the law would know about that route.

When Parker got off the plane in Great Falls, he was thinking the job was dead and the best thing for Wiss and Elkins to do was whack their former partners to keep from getting sold. Wiss waited for him outside, turning away as soon as he saw Parker, headed off for the short-term parking, but he didn't walk like a man with a sudden new set of troubles. Following, Parker wondered if maybe Wiss didn't know about Lloyd yet.

But he did. When Parker joined him in the car, a rental Taurus, he said, "You heard about Lloyd?"

Wiss grinned. "I sure did. From Larry himself."

"He came here?"

"He was already here when you called. I didn't want to say anything on the phone."

"What's the story?"

"He doesn't want to play footsie any more." Wiss seemed calm about it, driving them up route 87 toward Havre, but Parker had noted before that Wiss had taken a kind of mentor shine to Lloyd; maybe not a good thing.

Hunting season would start soon, and the road was dotted with SUVs full of guys wearing orange and red. Driving among them, looking like any other hunter, but not yet changed out of dark blue, Wiss said, "He saw his chance, deal with the guy messed him up, then forget the past, come out here. He figured to use his share of this thing to set himself up as Mister New."

"Not everybody can do that," Parker said.

"Oh, I know." Wiss grinned, driving around a little old lady doing her grocery shopping before hunting season started. "I couldn't, for one. But I think Larry could. Except now we got this complication."

Parker said, "Your old partners."

Wiss laughed, but shook his head. "I know what you

mean, I keep expecting them to show up, but they're
not as fucked over as Larry. If they've got a shot at
keeping the straight world, they'll take it. Not that
they *can't* show up, when you least want them."

Parker shrugged the ex-partners away, saying,
"What's the complication?"

"Yesterday," Wiss told him, "the lodge filled up with
law. Federal first, ATF, then state, then county."

"What the hell for?"

Wiss shook his head, but couldn't keep down a grin.
He was like somebody who'd made a bad-news predic-
tion, not wanting it to come true, and now it has, so he
wins by being right but he loses by being in the middle of the bad news. He said, "It's the firebreak thing
again. Remember, when we first described this setup,
we said it was a firebreak."

"I remember."

"We went in the first time," Wiss explained again,
"but we didn't get what we went in for, so then they upgraded their security, made it tougher."

"You said law."

"That's the other part of the firebreak," Wiss told
him. "The robbery attracted attention, it made somebody somewhere in law enforcement think there was
something more in there than Paxton Marino was
talking about. Let me tell you what happened."

"Go ahead."

"Those three paintings we recognized, when we
went into the secret rooms," Wiss said, "they were a
special order, we told you."

"Yeah."

"The customer was an art dealer down in Dallas named Horace Griffith," Wiss said. "We dealt with him before, he was always okay. This time it was to grab these three special pictures from this traveling museum show, a special order from a customer of his. He didn't say who *his* customer was, but we didn't care."

"Paxton Marino."

"Sure. Yesterday, Griffith shows up at the lodge with a bunch of empty wooden crates, just the right size to carry paintings."

"I get it," Parker said. "That's your firebreak again. Now they're gonna move the stuff."

"But they don't get a chance," Wiss told him. "Right after Griffith gets there the place fills up with ATF, maybe thirty, forty of them, you'd think they're after terrorists."

"But they're not."

"When Larry told us, we said, what are they doing there, and he said, 'They're looking for our paintings.'" Wiss laughed. "Is that a pisser? They're looking for *our* paintings. Larry's gonna be okay, Parker."

That didn't matter, not now. "But there isn't a job any more," Parker said, meaning, if the job did still exist, they'd have to think very hard, should Lloyd still exist.

"We don't know yet," Wiss said. "The general feeling is, let's stick around, see what happens next."

"Until when?"

"Until the dust settles." Wiss shrugged. "Who

knows, maybe they'll truck the pictures outa there, we can hijack them on the road, we're the only ones know what and where they are."

"Possible," Parker agreed.

"At this point," Wiss said, "everything's possible. Listen, I forgot to ask. Did you deal with that problem?"

"Yes," Parker said.

2

Happy hunting," the clerk said, handing over the key, and Parker said, "Thanks."

As they walked down the cold space between the maroon doors of the units and the cars parked out front, Wiss said, "She thinks we're hunters, getting ready for the season."

"Well, we are," Parker said, and stopped at his room, number eleven.

Pointing, Wiss said, "We're all connected, with doors in between. Frank's next, then me, then Larry."

"I'll unpack, then meet where?"

"My room," Wiss said, "it's handiest. Bring your chair, there's only one in each room."

Elkins' room was empty and very neat, as though the guest hadn't arrived yet. Elkins and Wiss were together in Wiss's room, playing cards. This place

looked more lived-in, maybe just because of the two
men with cards in their hands. All the interior doors
were open, and through the last one Parker could see
Lloyd seated cross-legged on the floor in there,
screens and keyboards and phones in a semicircle on
the floor around him, a set of thin black earphones on
his head, notepad in his lap, making notes.

Wiss looked up from his hand when Parker walked
in. Nodding his head at the dresser, he said, "Bourbon, ice bucket, plastic glasses."

Parker put his chair near the card players, then
crossed to the dresser, saying, "What's going on?"

"Larry's getting an update," Wiss told him.

Elkins played a card and said, "The feds are fighting
with Washington. The feds here, fighting with the feds
there." He glanced at Parker. "You know what they call
it? Washington? You know what the feds call Washington? Sog. Seat of government. Sog. English isn't good
enough for them."

Parker brought his glass back, sat beside the other
two, and said, "What are they arguing about?"

"The ones here," Elkins said, watching Wiss play,
"are absolutely sure there's something to find. Art.
Paintings. They think illegally in the country, maybe
Holocaust stuff, stolen by the Nazis. The feds *there* say,
where's your evidence? Where's your probable cause?
You are dealing with rich important people here, without a smirch on their character, don't step on your
dick out there."

Parker said, "You're saying, they can't find the hidden rooms."

"Not so far," Elkins agreed.

Wiss said, "But Larry says, they're looking for the architect. The main architect, there was more than one there. But the main one's supposed to be in San Francisco, his office is in San Francisco, but they think he's in Tokyo right now, on a project, or São Paulo."

Parker said, "Sooner or later, they'll find the plans. You can't hide— What did you say it was? Three rooms?"

"About this size," Wiss said. "About like going from you to Frank to me."

"So it could be a space forty by fifteen." Parker shook his head. "They can't not find that."

"Well, it's the basement," Elkins pointed out, "and it's modern architecture, you know, it isn't your basic shoebox, it's got funny angles, and not all of it has basement underneath, the way it's built into the side of the mountain."

"Also," Wiss said, "part of the job would have been to hide it, fool the eye, make it look as though there isn't any space unaccounted for."

"Still," Parker said, "they'll find it."

"It's looking like," Elkins said, "they're not gonna find it without the plans. And they may not be given the time. They been there since yesterday, it's getting to be an embarrassment, Sog wants them to pull out before the heavyweights start leaning on them."

"From what Larry's hearing," Wiss added, "Marino's

already got lawyers in DC bitching about this, pulling in markers from congressmen."

Lloyd came in from his room. "Welcome back," he said to Parker.

"You've been busy," Parker said.

Lloyd grinned, pleased with himself, then shrugged it off and said, "We've all been busy. The latest, the ATF talked to the FBI to get the Italian police to talk to Marino. They're setting up an appointment, in Milan, for tomorrow."

Elkins snorted. "These are cops," he asked, "when they want to talk to you, they give you an appointment?"

"When you got a billion dollars," Wiss commented, "you get an appointment."

Parker said, "So the law's going to be up there at least until tomorrow."

"That's the other thing," Lloyd said. He sat on the edge of Wiss's bed, the only one not drinking, and said, "They've given up looking. For now. So most of them are leaving, just two staying on, an ATF art specialist named Hayes and a state CID inspector named Moxon. And they're making the staff leave, too, closing the whole compound, nobody in, nobody out."

"Treating it like a crime scene," Wiss pointed out. "Secure the area, bring out the measuring tape and the Polaroid cameras."

"Two of the staff," Lloyd went on, "are going to be staying at this place here. Dave Rappleyea and Fred Wheeler."

Elkins found that amusing. "We're gonna be neighbors?"

"That's right," Lloyd said. "They're making them share a room, up on the second floor."

Elkins said, "Well, they're employees."

Wiss said, "What about Griffith?"

"He's going back to Dallas," Lloyd told him. "I think they'd have liked to keep him, but it isn't a federal offense to ship empty crates around."

Elkins said, "Are you hearing what his story is? Griffith; what's his explanation for the crates?"

"His story is, he doesn't know what they were for. Marino asked him to bring them up, but didn't say why, and Marino's a very good customer, so Griffith did what he wanted, and expected a phone call at the lodge to tell him what to do next."

Wiss said, "Now Marino's gonna talk to Italian cops. What story is *he* gonna tell?"

"He and Griffith are e-mailing each other all the time," Lloyd said, "but you know how secure that can be."

Elkins laughed. "For instance," he said, "*we're* reading it."

"Exactly. So they're being very circumspect, very careful what they say to each other. A lot of 'as you know' stuff."

Elkins said, "Are they on the same page yet?"

"The story's going to be," Lloyd told him, "Marino's moving some of his paintings, the ordinary ones out on the walls in the regular part of the lodge, he's gonna move some of them to his place in the Alps, but he didn't decide yet which ones, so he wanted a bunch of different-size crates."

Parker said, "Nobody's going to buy that, not in Italy and not here."

"They might in Sog," Elkins said. "Money's the only thing they really believe, down in Sog."

"It doesn't matter if they believe it," Lloyd said, "it only matters that it gives their lawyers something to say."

Parker said, "I'm trying to decide, is delay better for us, or worse? Do we still want to break in there, or hijack it on the road?"

Wiss said, "I think it's better where it is. We already know the layout. Also, they don't know yet what they're gonna find. Once they've got it, and see what it is, they'll *really* do tight security."

Elkins said, "So we've got until they find the architect."

"Well, a little longer," Lloyd told him. "Until they finish talking to the architect's lawyer."

"Then *we* should talk with our new neighbors," Parker said. "Make them feel at home. Dave Rappleyea and Fred Wheeler."

3

Parker watched Elkins introduce himself to Dave Rappleyea. He was good at that sort of thing, easygoing enough, not threatening, but also not overly hearty. Having a conversation with somebody who might know something useful in the heist you were working on was part of his job description: heavy lifting.

Rappleyea looked like a guy who didn't get into conversations with human beings very often. A pudgy sort in baggy jeans and a shapeless black V-neck sweater over a green T-shirt, he had long pale yellow hair, almost white, pulled back behind his ears from a central part, and he blinked out at the world through perfectly round tortoiseshell glasses.

Parker and Elkins and Wiss had trailed Rappleyea, and the other one, Fred Wheeler, to this bar-restaurant diagonally across the road from the motel. It was a squarish room, booths on both sides, tables in the middle, bar at the back, no nonsense about no smoking. It was maybe half full at seven on a Wednesday evening, most of the customers already dressed for hunting.

Rappleyea and Wheeler took a booth on the right, and Parker and Elkins and Wiss took the next one beyond them, Wiss with his back to Rappleyea so he could listen to their conversation, Parker and Elkins facing him so they could watch the other two.

But there was no conversation to listen to, and nothing interesting to watch. Rappleyea had some sort of handheld computer game he was playing, pausing only to order his dinner, then eating one-handed so he could continue to play with the other. Wheeler read a car magazine through his dinner, thoroughly, slowly, doggedly, as though he expected to be tested on it later. They didn't speak, didn't look at each other, barely admitted there was anyone else at the table.

Wheeler ate the way he read his magazine, doggedly and completely, and was finished first. "See you," he said—Rappleyea nodded, not looking up from his game—and got to his feet and left. Rappleyea was still eating, being slowed down by his one-handedness.

"This should be fun," Elkins said, and stood. He strolled over to the cash register, looked at the local-attraction brochures on the narrow shelves underneath it, chose one, and ambled back, nodding in pleased surprise over a color picture of a cataract somewhere in the Bear Paw Mountains. He started to slide into the next booth, across the table from Rappleyea, and as Rappleyea looked up, startled, Elkins showed his own surprise and embarrassment as he hastily got up again, saying, "Oops, sorry, wrong booth. I'm back there."

"Okay," said Rappleyea, and looked down at his game.

Which Elkins pointed at, saying, "Is that a Game-Boy?"

"No, it's a Q-Pac," Rappleyea said, not quite looking up.

Elkins said, "What, is that better?"

"It's different, that's all." Rappleyea finally gave Elkins complete eye contact, holding up the computer game as he said, "You can play it with one hand, if you're busy doing something else."

"Well, that's pretty good," Elkins agreed. "Listen, are you from around here? Do you know any white-water rafting we could drive to?"

"No, I'm sorry, I'm not local, I wouldn't—"

"Oh, sure, that's right, I saw you over at the motel. I'm from Chicago myself, near Chicago. Where do you live?"

Rappleyea fumbled with this rapid-fire dialogue, saying, "Well, I— I *live* here now, well, I don't exactly; I've got a job here."

"Much industry in these parts?" Elkins asked. "I thought it was mostly scenic, and hunting, and like that. You a guide?"

"No, I . . ." Rappleyea was stuck, involved deeper in

conversation than he could handle. Elkins waited, smiling, friendly, interested without being intrusive, not pushing his new friend, and finally Rappleyea said, "I'm working security, up at a lodge near here."

"A lodge," Elkins echoed. "Like a hotel?"

"No, it's private, it's a real rich guy, he's almost never there, it's just us security people in the place."

"Sounds like a cushy job," Elkins commented. "How come they make you live in the motel?"

"Oh, that's just temporary," Rappleyea said. His left hand still held the game, but it was obvious he'd pretty much forgotten about it. He said, "We had a robbery, a while ago, and the police want to—"

"A robbery!" Elkins was delighted. "Up at this rich man's place? They get much?"

"No, the alarms went off, they got caught. Some of them got caught."

"*You* caught 'em," Elkins suggested, grinning, pointing at Rappleyea.

"Well, not all by myself." Clearly, Rappleyea was enjoying being the center of somebody else's attention.

"How come you let some of them get away?" Elkins demanded, then laughed, and said, "No, I'm kidding." Sticking out his hand, he said, "Frank Emerson, that's me."

"Hi." Rappleyea awkwardly shook hands. "Dave Rappleyea."

"Nice to know you, Dave. Listen, I'm with my pals at this booth right here, why don't you come join us?"

"Oh, I couldn't horn in on . . ." Rappleyea said, the

words fading into a mumble as he snuck a quick glance at his game.

Elkins said, "Why not? Come on, we'd love to have you." Moving toward the next booth, he said, very cheerful, to Parker and Wiss, "They had a big robbery up where this guy works, can you believe it? A peaceful part of the world like this? Come on, Dave, meet the guys."

"Well . . . okay," Rappleyea said. With a shy but happy grin, he slid out of the booth. His face was pinker than before.

In the next forty-five minutes, he told them everything they needed to know.

4

On the one hand," Elkins said, "it's tougher, because now the law is there, and they know there's something to look for, and they're looking for it. On the other hand, it's easier, because there's only the two guys up there, no eyes to watch the monitors."

"They're in the lodge," Parker pointed out. "Not in the staff house. They're sitting in there on top of the paintings."

Lloyd said, "With full communication with the outside world."

"Sog," Elkins commented.

"Not just Washington," Lloyd told him. "They're in touch with the state police in Helena, and the local police in Havre."

They had brought all four chairs into Wiss's room in the motel, but none of them were seated. It was after eleven at night, the television in Wiss's room was on to the news with the sound turned off—just in case a picture of the lodge or somebody connected to it would appear—and they were deciding how to deal with the changed playing field. They all paced while they talked, stopped or walked while they listened.

Parker said, "We've got to go in there soon. It isn't gonna get better up there. In the next day or two, they'll find the architect, they'll get their hands on the plans, they'll figure them out, they'll find that little private gallery, they'll call in the choppers."

"We're not gonna do it tonight," Elkins said.

Lloyd said, "We almost could. It's quieter up there than it's been for quite a while."

Parker said, "What about daytime?"

"When they see us coming," Wiss said, "they call for reinforcements."

"They've still got those lights," Elkins pointed out, "they'll see us no matter what time we come in, and that's the time they'll make their call." He turned to Lloyd. "What can you do about that?"

Lloyd shrugged, as though the answer were easy. "Divert," he said.

Wiss said, "Larry? What do you mean, divert?"

"It's the equivalent of a wiretap," Lloyd told him. "In the old days, you'd just tap a phone, listen in, that's all there is to it. Once the fax came along, they had to work up a technology so they could divert the incoming fax to their own machine, print it out, then send it on where it was supposed to go in the first place, without any footprints on it from the diversion.

The feds were doing that with the stock market swindlers for a long time before anybody caught on. And now the same kind of concept works for e-mail. Divert it so you can read it, then send it on as though nothing had happened, with only the original sender's track on it."

Elkins said, "What good does that do us?"

"Up till now," Lloyd said, "I've been diverting, then sending on, because all I wanted was to read what everybody had to say. Now, I don't send it on."

Wiss grinned. "Like shutting off a faucet," he said.

"Something like that," Lloyd agreed. "And from now on, if an answer is needed, I put together the answer myself, using all their passwords and technical footprints from their previous messages."

Parker said, "So that's what you can do. If they send out an SOS, it comes to you and nobody else."

"By any means they want to try," Lloyd said.

Elkins said, "Except smoke signal."

"That's somebody else's department," Lloyd agreed.

Parker said, "And the answer to the SOS they get is from you, but they think it's from their friends."

"Exactly," Lloyd said. "They say SOS, strangers approaching the lodge, I say help is on the way."

"Then we go in," Parker said, "and they don't send any more messages."

"But *I* do," Lloyd said. "They're making hourly reports, up to eleven at night and starting at eight in the morning, what they're doing, what they found, what the situation is. Nobody wants to feel isolated up there, so they're in touch with every level of command from Havre to DC."

Wiss said to Parker, "And Larry does that, too, sends in the reports, long as we need to."

Parker said, "Tomorrow morning, we buy orange coats. Tomorrow afternoon, we go hunting."

5

At quarter after one the next afternoon, Parker and Elkins and Wiss climbed out of their gray Jeep at the top of Marino's road by the shack, well above the lodge. All three wore bright orange coats, red and black wool hats with earlaps, black corduroy pants, and tall brown boots. All three wore, in their right ears, under the earlap, a small transmitter from which the tinny voice of Lloyd spoke to them from time to time, down in his room at the motel in Chinook. Hooked to the underpart of the rigid brims of their caps were small microphones, so they could talk back to Lloyd. All three had Remington .35s broken open over their forearms, and fake hunting licenses in clear plastic packs fastened like targets to the backs of their orange coats. All three had black moustaches and black-framed eyeglasses.

"We're starting down now," Elkins said.

Lloyd's little voice, like a leprechaun in the ear, said, "Is it cold?"

Wiss, embarrassed for his protégé, sounded irritated instead, saying, "Of course it's cold, Larry. We're not here to chitchat."

"Sorry."

It was cold enough to see your icy breath, cold enough to make the gloves they wore necessary, though the gloves might cause a little trouble if they had to use the Remingtons. They walked down the paved road, ice crystals crackling with a dry rustle beneath their boots. Ahead the sentry towers loomed, lights off but cameras still on, looking inward.

"Frank!"

Not Lloyd, not the voice in the ear, but someone behind them. Parker and the others spun around, and a guy was there, on the road a few yards uphill from them, holding his arms well out to the sides, palms forward, to show he was unarmed. He was in a black pea jacket and black wool cap, a bulky guy, probably in his late thirties, with a big heavy-boned face.

Sounding astonished, and not happy, Elkins said, "Bob! For Christ's sake—"

"Don't worry about us," Bob said, patting the air to calm everybody down, while the voice in Parker's ear asked, "What's happening? Bob? Who's Bob?" Nobody was going to answer Larry, because nobody was going to tell Bob there was another pair of ears here.

Elkins said, "They're gonna revoke your parole, Bob." He really didn't want this guy here.

"They did, yesterday," Bob told him. "I said to you, it was taking too long, Frank. Harry and me took off, so where else we gonna go?"

Wiss, sounding like a stern parent, said, "Not here, Bob."

"We won't horn in on you, honest to God," Bob said. "It's your play. Just so you know, Harry and me, we'll be up by your car. You need a hand, you can count on us. You want us out, we're out."

"We want you farther out than this, Bob," Wiss said.

Bob shrugged, turning mulish. "Well, this is the way the hand plays," he said. "We'll stay up there till it's over, we'll help if we're needed, we'll divvy when it's done, you go your way, we'll go ours."

Larry in the earphone had grown silent, so he'd caught up with what was happening. Wiss and Elkins looked at each other, then at Parker. Parker thought somebody around here wouldn't live through the day; too many people coming from too many angles. He said, "It's okay. They'll stay up there, on deck."

"That's right," Bob said, and tried to toss a manly smile in Parker's direction. "Thanks, pal."

Parker shrugged. He said, "Come on," and turned away, walking downhill again. After a second, the other two followed, looking back uphill at Bob, who waved to them, then turned away, going back up the road toward his partner, Harry.

Parker and Elkins and Wiss walked on down past the ring of camera towers. Anybody watching? No. Still no. Occasionally, it seemed to Parker, he could hear

Lloyd's breath in his ear, but nothing else. The man didn't hum or whistle on the job.

"Gotcha!"

The three kept walking, didn't break stride. Wiss said, "Larry? They see us?"

"Picked you up on the perimeter cameras, now they're phoning Havre. Hold on."

The three kept walking, not on the road but paralleling it, looking around as though for game. Two minutes later, Larry's voice said, "They're confused, because this is Thursday and the season doesn't start till Monday. They think you're jumping the season on purpose, you probably figure to be alone up there, maybe you're down from Canada."

Elkins said, "What do they plan to do about it?"

"Nothing, unless you approach the house."

"I see the house now," Wiss said.

They slowed, moving toward the lodge. The people inside were lawmen, and so would ask questions first. But the image they should be given was of dumbass hunters, maybe half-smart wiseguys looking to make a kill before it was legal. They should not be given an image of people stalking the lodge with robbery in mind.

"Angle to the right," Parker said, "as though we meant to go around the house."

They could see it clearly now, looming ahead of them through the trees, gleaming white in the world of gray and brown and dark green. The two lawmen inside were not visible, but were certainly watching the three orange coats approach.

Wiss said, "Larry, the next message you get, divert."

"Oh, I know. Nothing happening now, though."

Parker said, "We should stop here, talk it over among ourselves, point different directions, discuss which way we want to go."

They did that, and then Parker pointed toward the house, saying, "Now I'm saying maybe we should go see if somebody's home."

Wiss and Elkins looked toward the house. Elkins said, "And we're talking it over, do they know much about hunting around here?"

Wiss said, "We're wondering, will they help us, or call the cops?"

They looked at one another, and shrugged, and moved their arms around. "And now," Parker said, "we're deciding what the hell, let's just go over there and knock on the door."

They all nodded at one another, then moved to- ward the house, angling first to get back onto the paved road, then walking downhill.

"That's far enough, fellas."

The loudspeaker had a brassy loud twang to it, and seemed to be coming from the trees all around them, not from the house at all. The three stopped and looked around.

"This is private property. Move outside the perimeter of the towers."

The three turned to one another. Parker angled

himself so his face was away from the lodge as he said, "They might have a directional mike in there."

Elkins, sounding aggrieved, said, "I don't see why we can't just *ask*. It wouldn't kill them to be friendly."

"Besides," Wiss said, "my own opinion is, we're kinda lost."

Parker turned to face the lodge. "Well," he said, "if we just keep going downhill, we'll get to the road some time or other."

Wiss said, "But *where* on the road? This thing isn't panning out at all."

"Move along, fellas."

"Screw this," Elkins said. "What are they gonna do, shoot me? I'll be right back." He took a step toward the house, then stopped and said, "Jesus, wait a minute, I'm carrying a rifle." Turning, he extended the Remington to Wiss, saying, "Here, you hold it for me."

"Sure."

Without the rifle, Elkins started toward the lodge again, and made about half the distance before the door over there opened. This north side of the lodge featured a wide white door, heavily framed with half columns. Leading to it were four broad shallow wooden steps, gray-painted, up from where the road curved around close to the house before circling it to meet the even more elaborate entrance at the front.

This entrance was elaborate enough, with plenty of room on the top step for the guy who now came out, looking stern. He was a tall man, not heavy, and wore what seemed like a military greatcoat in dark blue over a flannel shirt and blue jeans. A dark blue hard-billed officer's cap was on his head. So this would be the state CID inspector, casual in the house, putting on his official wear to repel the interlopers. Pointing a rigid finger at Elkins, he said, "This is a restricted area, my friend. Move along *out* of here."

Instead of which, Elkins kept moving forward. He was about twenty yards from the CID man now, not hurrying, closing the gap. Behind him, Parker and Wiss also moved forward, more slowly. Holding his hands out, Elkins said, "Mister, this isn't a very friendly way to treat a fella. We're just trying to—"

"*Stop* right there," the CID man said. "I am a peace officer, and I am ordering you off this property."

"Listen," Elkins said, still moving forward, "if you're a lawman, that's fine, here, I'll show you my ID," reaching in under the orange coat, on the right side, toward his back pants pocket, "my friends and me are just up here to"—bringing out the Colt Super Auto .38, suddenly rushing forward, Parker and Wiss coming fast—"*keep* your hands where I can see them or you're a fucking *dead* man! *Back! Back! Back!*" Crowding the astonished CID man back across the broad top step toward the open door.

"You mean— You can't—"

"Moxon!" Elkins shouted, using the CID man's name to give him a second shock. "Shut up and listen! You want to stay alive!"

All four crowded through the doorway, Moxon

backward, the color draining from his face. He was a craggy rangy man, a little over the hill, who kept himself in shape and hadn't known anything like this could happen to him.

Parker's gloves were off now, the Remington cocked as he pushed it past Elkins into Moxon's stomach, saying, "Call Hayes. Tell him to show his face."

"I—I'm alone here," Moxon stammered.

Elkins slapped Moxon's military hat off with the barrel of the automatic. He was the one being dangerous, unpredictable. "Do we look stupid?" he demanded. "We know your names, the two of you."

Wiss shut the door, and Parker poked Moxon in the stomach again with the barrel of the Remington. "It's just as easy for us," he said, "we work in here, without you alive."

"Easier," Elkins said, and laid the automatic against Moxon's left cheek.

"There are law officers," Moxon said, and started again, "this is secure, there are law officers all over this mountain."

Parker said, "That's how we got in here." He looked past Moxon at the room, a large, broad, wood-walled place with brick floor and brass wall sconces, several coats hanging on a row of wooden dowels along the back, over a broad rough-timber bench, boots of various kinds under the bench, wide doorways open on both sides. He called, "Hayes! Come out now, or we shoot Moxon, and then come in for you."

Lloyd's little voice said, "I just told him help's on the way."

Elkins laughed. "Come out, Hayes!" he cried. "You're done with your phone call! Oley oley in free!"

Moxon, sounding worried, said, "Phone call?"

Wiss stood to one side, his Remington loose in his hands, pointed at the brick floor. He was the calm one. "It was a friend of ours," he said, "who just told Hayes that help was on the way. He lied. Every message you send out of here, phone, e-mail, whatever you want, goes to our friend and nobody else."

"So there's no reason to stall," Parker said.

Moxon looked at him. He considered Parker's face a long time, not as though to remember it for some lineup farther down the road but as though to read the truth there, whatever it might turn out to be. Then, still looking at Parker, he angled his head back a bit and called, "Bert, come on out. The criminals have returned to the scene of the crime."

6

The second lawman was also in jeans and flannel shirt and boots. This one, Bert Hayes from Washington, was a sandy-haired, short, angry-looking man in his mid-forties who came through the doorway on the right with his hands held out in front of himself, arms spread wide and palms forward, not as though he were surrendering or showing himself without weapons but as though he were making a point in an ongoing argument: *You see? You understand now?* What he said, in a raspy aggravated voice, was, "There isn't one fucking thing you people are going to accomplish around here."

Parker stepped back, to cover them both with the Remington. With a look at Elkins and a nod toward the lawmen, he said, "De-fang."

"Right."

Elkins went in a half-circle, to get around Moxon and

Hayes without being in the line of fire from either Wiss
or Parker. Putting his own .38 away, he patted down first
Moxon, finding a small hip-holster pistol, and then
Hayes, bringing out another small pistol, this one from
an ankle holster. "That's all."

Parker said, "No cuffs?"

"No." Elkins shrugged. "There's closets."

Moxon, sounding surprisingly mild beside the glowering Hayes, said, "You're the people who broke in last
time."

Grinning, Elkins said, "Naw. We just saw your light."

"The thing is," Moxon said, "there's a hidden room
in this place somewhere, and we've been going nuts trying to find it."

"Three rooms," Wiss said.

Both lawmen were surprised at that. "There can't
be," Hayes said. "That's like hiding a tank in your back-
yard."

Moxon said, "I'm beginning to think you people've
been keeping tabs on us."

Parker wanted to get this thing moving. He said,
"What's your point?"

"You'll lock us in a room or tie us up or whatever,"
Moxon said. "I don't think you'll kill a peace officer if
you don't have to, and you won't have to, and you figure those moustaches and glasses can confuse identification just enough, so we'll cooperate. If we see a
chance in our favor, naturally, we'll take it."

"Fucking A," Hayes said.

Wiss said, "That's all we'd expect. You take care of yourselves, we take care of ourselves, nobody gets hurt."

"All I ask," Moxon said, "is to know where the hidey-hole is."

Elkins laughed. "It really got to you," he said.

Wiss said, "That's okay. Somewhere down there is where we'd stash you anyway." Looking at Parker, seeing his impatience, he said, "It's okay. It keeps everybody calm, and it moves us along. We're going down there anyway."

"Then let's go."

Moxon and Hayes looked at Elkins, who said, "We come in last time from the other side. There's a hall off a big dining room, with a flight of stairs down to the basement."

"We've been down there a lot," Moxon said.

Elkins said, "Well, we'll go again. You first, then me, then Bert, then my friends."

Moxon nodded, and they trooped through the house, all white and pale green and gold, more Versailles than hunting lodge, and down the broad wood stairs to the carpeted main room of the basement, where the empty wooden cartons to transport the paintings leaned in a row against the wall. Open doorways to left and right showed storage rooms full of magpie keepings. Soft fluorescent ceiling lights gave an even greenish gold illumination.

When they were all down the stairs, Elkins said to Moxon, "Come on over here. Stand right there. Look at the carpet. Along there."

Moxon, not knowing what he was supposed to be looking at, stood where Elkins had put him and frowned at the floor. He switched his frown to Elkins, who only grinned at him and raised an eyebrow, and then he frowned at the floor again, until all at once his eyes widened and he said, "Son of a bitch!"

"Roy?" Hayes said. "What is it?"

Moxon said to Elkins, "Can he have a look?"

"Sure," Elkins said. "It's a bonus prize."

Parker wanted to get moving here, but he knew what Elkins was doing, and why. Keep the customer calm, keep him from feeling desperate, from feeling he *has* to find a way out of this. It would pay off later, but it was an irritation now.

Hayes moved over to stand where Moxon had been, with Moxon now just to his left, but no matter how long Hayes glared at the floor he didn't see what the others were talking about until Moxon gently said, "Bert, look at the nap of the carpet. Look at the line."

"Well, Jesus Christ," Hayes said, seeing it at last. "It's a goddam Indian trail!" He looked at the blank wall where the trail stopped. "That's supposed to be mountain back there," he said. "Solid rock."

"It's solid, all right," Elkins said, and in Parker's ear Lloyd's tinny voice said, "We got trouble."

Parker and Elkins and Wiss all got very alert. Parker said, "What trouble?"

Moxon and Hayes looked at him, not getting it, while Lloyd said, "There's an FBI man in Dallas has to talk to Hayes."

"Dallas," Elkins said. "Griffith."

The lawmen turned now to look at Elkins.

Lloyd said, "I've been deflecting him, trouble on the line, but it won't work much longer. Anything else I can deal with, but not a phone call."

Parker said to Elkins, "Speakerphone."

Elkins shrugged. "I wouldn't know."

Parker turned to Moxon and Hayes. "You'll know," he said. "And this is your chance to keep yourself alive."

"There's an office by the front door," Moxon said, "has a speakerphone."

"I remember that room," Wiss said.

Parker said, "That's where we go."

The five trooped upstairs, in the same order as before, and turned toward the front of the house, as Lloyd's voice sounded in Parker's ear, now with a trace of panic: "This guy's talking about sending state troopers from Havre. I've really got to let him through."

"Two minutes," Parker told him. "Can you change your voice? Be your own supervisor."

"Oh, God, I don't know," Lloyd said. "Let me see what I can do."

The five walked through the ground floor of the sprawling house, coming at last to a good-sized office with copier and computer and wall maps of the area and a large partner's desk with a green felt inlaid top and antique swivel chairs on both sides, and the phone. They all crowded in, and Parker said to Elkins, "Take Roy into the hall, sit him on the floor where we can see him. If you hear one wrong word from Bert, shoot off his basket." Turning, he said, "Bert, move that chair back from the desk, middle of the room. When the phone rings, answer it, put it on speaker *then*, come sit down in the chair."

"Who's calling me?" Hayes asked, as Elkins positioned Moxon outside the door.

"He'll tell you," Parker said, and told Lloyd, "We're ready."

Lloyd must have been busy with the call from Dallas, because he didn't answer, but less than a minute later the phone chirped. With an eye on Parker, Hayes picked up the receiver, said, "Hayes," then, "Hold on, let me put you on the speaker."

He pushed that button, hung up, and stepped back toward the desk chair in the middle of the room as a metallic voice filled the space: "I think we may be buying a break at last in this thing."

Hayes rubbed his forehead. He seemed uncertain what to do. From where he sat, he could see the phone, he could see Moxon seated on the floor in the front hall and Elkins holding the Remington on him, and he could see Wiss and Parker both pointing pistols at his own head.

The metallic voice said, "You there?"

Hayes sighed. "Sorry," he said. "You were agent— agent—"

"Catlett. You still having phone trouble there?"

"Uhh . . . We been having phone trouble?"

"I've been trying to reach you people fifteen, twenty minutes."

"I had no idea."

"Well, here's the thing. The antique dealer Griffith, that you had up your way for a while?"

"Yeah?"

"He's on his way to Austin right now, with his lawyer, to make a statement."

Hayes made a what-now shrug toward Moxon and said, "What kind of statement?"

Agent Catlett said, "His lawyer contacted the federal prosecutor in Dallas this morning, floated the idea of Griffith flipping. He'll give us Marino, who it looks like has been doing a lot of stuff he shouldn't, if there's no jail time in it for Griffith."

Hayes said, "Can they make that deal?"

"Nobody knows yet," Catlett said, "but nobody really needs to lean on Griffith, he's just the errand boy, so it should be able to work. And it looks like it would include the whereabouts of Marino's stash up there, that room nobody can find."

Hayes and Moxon exchanged a look. "That's great news," Hayes said, but he didn't sound sincere.

Catlett apparently didn't hear the hollowness in Hayes's answer. He said, "We're anticipating the deal with Griffith will work out. We've already asked the Italian police to hold on to Marino, and we've got evidence people on the way to you right now from Helena, should be there by two this afternoon."

Three hours.

Hayes said, "Looking forward to them. Who's in charge?"

"Inspector Winnick. One of yours, from ATF."

"I know Winnick," Hayes said. "Be happy to see him."

"In the meantime," Catlett said, "the bureau thinks it's best you make contact with the state police in Havre, ask them to send some people up, secure the area."

Parker pointed at Hayes, and shook his head.

Hayes said, "Is that really necessary? Inspector Moxon and I pretty well have the place under control."

"It's no reflection on you," Catlett assured him. "Sog just wants to nail it down, now that we've got Griffith turning."

With a helpless shrug toward Parker, Hayes said, "Well, if that's the decision."

"A state CID man named Elwood is in Havre now," Catlett said, "waiting for your call."

"Then I'd better call him," Hayes said. "Thanks for the heads-up."

"My pleasure," Catlett said.

Parker stepped forward and hit the button to end the call. They all looked at one another.

Moxon said, "I'm sorry, friends, but your parade has been cancelled."

7

Parker, moving, said, "Bert, on your feet, into the hall. Roy, stay on the floor, down on your face. Bert, beside him. Hands behind your backs."

They both obeyed, though Moxon mildly said, "It's no good, you know. Another couple minutes, nobody's heard from us, nobody can get through, they'll be right up here. You don't have three hours."

"That's my problem," Parker told him. Holding the Remington one-handed, he pointed at Wiss: "Tie them." Pointed at Elkins: "Get your friends and the car. Tell them what's going on."

Neither Wiss nor Elkins bothered to speak. Wiss went to one knee between the two prone men, drawing lengths of household electric cord from his pocket, tying wrists and then ankles. He started with Moxon, who lay silent, having already made the point he wanted to make. Hayes, when Wiss started, said, "Jesus, that's *tight!*"

"Has to be, to be any good," Wiss told him. "Everybody knows that."

As Wiss got to his feet, Parker gestured to him to move away down the hall. He left the Remington, leaning it against the wall, then said, as they walked, "How long to get into the gallery?"

Wiss looked very doubtful. "Oh, man, with this time pressure? We should've brought grenades."

"We're not leaving here empty-handed," Parker told him, "and we're not carrying out gold toilets."

"So we'll take a look at it."

As they hurried down the basement stairs, Wiss said, "Last time, once we found the door and busted into it, turned out, it had a kind of electric lock on it, you'd use a remote like for a garage door, but we didn't see any remote. Well, we didn't look that much, we were already in there by then."

They stood by the wall where the faint trail in the carpet ended. It was featureless, extending ten feet from a corner rightward to the entrance to the wine cellar, a deep narrow parquet-floored room with bottles in copper racks on the left side and a combination of racks and refrigerators on the right. Beyond the depth of a wine bottle, on the left, was the side wall to the gallery area.

Standing in the wine cellar doorway, Parker said, "It could be anything. It has to be near, but it could be anything. It could be one of those bottles, it could be you

step on one special parquet tile. Or it could be something in one of these other storage rooms all around
here."

"That's why we went in hard last time," Wiss said.
Upstairs, a phone rang. "I was supposed to have an
hour, two hours, this time around. This isn't breaking
a window."

Parker moved slowly along the blank wall, sliding
his hand along it. "I can feel the seam," he said. "You
can't see it, but you can feel it."

"A beautiful snug fit," Wiss said. "You gotta admire
the workmanship."

"Can you make a hole in it?"

Wiss brought a small portable drill out of his orange
coat, felt the wall, found the seam, and the drill started
to whine. Ten seconds later Wiss stopped, shaking his
head, stepping back. "No good," he said. Upstairs, the
phone still rang. "Last time, the door was metal, but
not like this. This, under the paint here, this is stainless steel."

"The wall beside it?"

The drill whined again, and again Wiss stepped
back. "Concrete," he said. The phone had stopped
ringing. "If I had half an hour," Wiss said, "I could
make a hole. An hour to get in." He looked disgusted.
"We came a long way, Parker," he said, "but we ain't
getting in there."

The job was going to hell. Law coming, law in resi-
dence, Griffith the potential customer talking to the

prosecutors, and a stainless-steel door. "Your firebreak works," Parker said.

Wiss said, "Larry?"

They listened to nothing. Parker said, "He's gone."

"Well," Wiss said, "he's right."

Parker said, "I know he is. Come on."

They turned toward the stairs, and Wiss said, "There'll be some swag in the house, pay our expenses."

"Hold it right there."

They stopped, both looking up, and slowly down the stairs came Elkins, looking disgusted. Behind him, peering over his shoulder, was the guy who'd braced them up by the car. Bob. Up there, he'd been everybody's pal, just going to wait up there, not horn in on anybody's play, just wait for his former partners Wiss and Elkins to get into the lodge and back out. Now he was something else, tense and wary, crouched behind Elkins, left hand on Elkins' left shoulder, right hand showing a Colt automatic next to Elkins' right ear, the two of them stopped halfway down the stairs. "Just hold it there," Bob repeated. "Ralph? You through that door?"

"Can't be done, Bob," Wiss said.

Parker took a step sideward, away from Wiss, but Bob reacted big to the movement, waggling the Colt, saying, "No no, pal, stay right there, I like you two together." To Wiss he said, "Whadaya mean, you can't? That's our money in there, too, you know. Or did you decide, it's easier, just get rid of Harry and me."

Not answering that, Wiss said, "It's stainless steel, Bob, in a concrete wall. We don't have the *time*. We got cops coming."

"Like I told him," Elkins said. He sounded as disgusted as he looked.

Bob said, "Not good enough, Ralph. Harry and me, we broke bail, we're hangin in space out here, we *need* that stake."

Parker said, "We'll leave it to you, it's all yours."

"Har, har," Bob said, not as though anything were funny. "Ralph's the lockman, aren't you, Ralph? Get through the fucking door!"

"I'll never do it before the cops get here," Wiss said.

"Then Harry and me, we're fucked anyway," Bob told him, "we're going down anyway, might as well have you guys for company." He gave Elkins a slight push, to encourage him to go down to the foot of the stairs. "Here's the situation," he said. "Harry's upstairs. He hears a shot, that means you birds probably outdrew me, so anybody goes up these stairs is dead. So you're here, until that door opens or the law walks in, so Ralph, you oughta quit wasting time."

Wiss gave Parker a helpless look. Parker, calm, said, "Go ahead, Ralph. Give it your best try. That's all right, just do it." Looking up at Bob, who had now seated himself on the sixth stair, he said, "Okay if I walk around? My rifle's upstairs, my pistol's in my coat pocket, I get the picture. It doesn't help me to shoot you."

The whine of Wiss's drill started again. Over it, Bob

said to Parker, "I don't care what you do, just so Ralph's getting us in at those paintings."

"Fine."

Elkins hovered over Wiss, wanting to help. Parker walked around the large room, looking in the open doorways at the storage areas. At one point, when he got a little too close to the stairs, Bob reared back, lifting his Colt, saying, "You don't have to come over here."

"Okay," Parker said, backing away. He'd seen to the top of the stairs, and the doorway was empty up there. Harry was hanging back, eyeballing the upper doorway without putting himself at risk from below.

Moving off from the staircase, Parker pointed at one of the open side doors. "Okay if I go in there? It's all sports gear, maybe they got a pair of gloves I can use."

Bob laughed. "Go ahead. You want gloves? Take 'em all." Nodding toward Wiss, where he labored at the door, he said, "I'm an art lover, myself."

8

Parker walked into a large square room lined with deep tall shelves and with stacks of sports equipment in neat piles in the middle of the floor. What he'd seen in here that had drawn him in was a large round red-bull's-eye target, straw-stuffed, on a wooden easel, leaning against shelves at the back of the room. What did Marino and his friends use to shoot at that target?

His first walk around the room, scanning the shelves, came up with nothing. Back in the doorway, he called to Wiss, "How's it coming?"

"Slow," Wiss said. He sounded almost tearful with frustration.

Bob, in good humor, looked over from watching the work to call, "You find your gloves?"

"Not yet."

Parker went back into the room, for another circuit, slower, looking deeper into all the shelves. There was

almost no time left. If this didn't pan out, he'd just
have to shoot the bastard, go up the stairs, and see
what happened.

There. Feathers. Neat feathers along a narrow
wooden stick. Parker moved two sets of ski poles out of
the way, and there was the quiver, tan, canvas, faked up
with Indian motifs, containing half a dozen arrows.
And next to it the bow.

When he slid the bow out from the shelf, it was a
very hard stiff wood, almost black, nearly four feet
long, carved into a graceful complex shape that
looked like an Arabic letter or a symbol on a sheet of
music. The bowstring was only fastened at one end,
and hung too short. It wasn't an ordinary cord but a
kind of cable, many threads wound together to make
something hard and strong.

Parker glanced over at the door, but couldn't see
the stairs from here. He put the end of the bow where
the string was attached onto the floor, against his in-
step, and bent the wood down until he could put the
loop at the top end of the string over the tip of the
bow into the nock.

Had he ever shot one of these things? If he had, he
couldn't remember it, but it wasn't high technology.
He selected one of the arrows, which also had a nock
at the back end of the shaft, beyond the feathers,
which the bowstring nestled into. He wrapped his left
hand around the bow's grip, rested the arrow's shaft
on top of his fist, and worked out how to hold the
arrow with the fingers of his right hand. Something

like a pool cue grip seemed right, between the feathers and the nock.

When he tried drawing the bowstring back, it was surprisingly taut. If he managed to let the thing go in the proper way, it would move with a hell of a force, but he could see how easy it would be to flub it, and have the arrow dribble away across the floor, asking a bullet to come rushing back.

There was no way to do practice shots. But there was nothing else to do either, except be gunned down either by Bob's friend Harry or by the law.

Parker moved up to the wall just to the left of the doorway. If he moved forward, he would see Bob diagonally across the room, seated on the sixth step, leaning back against the seventh step and the side wall, half-turned toward Parker, Colt in lap, eyes on Wiss and Elkins.

Parker inhaled, and held it. He drew the string back to his ear, left arm out straight as he held the bow. He stepped into the doorway, aimed down the shaft, opened his right hand. The arrow streaked across the space like an angry wasp and pinned Bob's chest to the wall.

9

Bob was trying to move, trying to breathe, trying to live. Wiss stopped the drill to gape at the arrow Bob was feebly fumbling at. Parker, dropping the bow and crossing the main room in long strides, pointed at Wiss, at the drill, made spinning motions with that hand. Wiss blinked, and pulled the trigger, and drilled air.

Parker reached Bob, looked up at the empty doorway at the top of the stairs, and still looking there closed his left hand on Bob's windpipe, squeezing in from both sides. Bob, in shock, bleeding inside, tried to fight away from him, but Parker leaned his weight on that hand, pressing the throat and head harder against the side wall, until the struggle lessened, then stopped.

Parker held for another long minute, then reached down to take the Colt out of Bob's lap. The blood that had started to seep from his mouth had stopped now, because the heart wasn't beating.

While the drill whirred in Wiss's hand behind him, Parker went slowly up the stairs. At the top, he waited, chest down on the stair edges, listening. What he could see was a trapezoid of hallway, pale green wall, part of a hunting scene genre painting, part of a many-bulbed golden chandelier.

Which way was the other one? If he committed to look to the left, and Harry was to the right, he'd be rewarded with a bullet in the head. He listened, the drill-whine only a faint burr behind him now, hoping to hear Harry breathe, or move, or yawn.

Nothing. How far away was he?

Fifty-fifty odds were not acceptable. Holding the Colt in his right hand, he reached into his left pants pocket. The only coin he ever carried while working was one quarter, in case he found himself in a place where he needed a phone. Now he took the quarter out and flipped it high and arcing across the hallway to flash glittering in the chandelier light, clink against the far wall, bounce silently on the carpeted floor.

A quick rustle; to the right; Parker launched himself out of the stairwell, diving as though into a swimming pool, right arm extended to the right, firing the Colt before he could see, landing flat on his chest, head to the right, sighting along his extended arm now at the bulky figure shooting, the gnats whizzing just above his head, firing the Colt, squeezing it off, squeezing it off, the figure bouncing back, half-turning, suddenly running away down the hall, Parker sending the rest of the Colt's clip after him, but the stance too awkward down here, no good at the increasing distance, Harry to the end of the hallway and through the door there and out of sight.

Feet under him, Colt tossed away, Parker called down, "Come up!" and ran down the hall as he pulled his own .38 revolver out of his coat pocket.

He could hear Wiss and Elkins behind him, but couldn't see Harry ahead. He had to slow at the doorway, hesitate, come in fast and low, see no one in the long dining room, the table like a bowling alley lane, the high-backed wooden chairs, the wall of mirrors under the chandeliers reflecting him back as he pursued down the long room and out the far end.

Every doorway was a delay, but every room he went into was empty, and at the end the rear door was open, the door he and the others had first come in. Parker raced through that doorway, out to the cold bright sunless northern day, and the bulky figure was getting into the Cherokee, their car that they'd left up above, that Elkins and the other two had driven down.

They *needed* that car. Parker fired, shattering the driver's window as Harry ducked, starting the engine, the Jeep jerking forward.

Parker fired again, but there was too little to shoot at. He didn't want to put out tires, hit the gas tank. The only target he was interested in was the man, but the man was too encased in the thick frame of the

Cherokee, and now it was moving away, cutting across the frozen lawn to turn back north.

Wiss and Elkins came panting out of the house, both with their guns in their hands. Wiss said, "What do we—" and they all heard the siren.

Sirens. They all faded back into the house, and two state police cars, red lights whirling on their roofs, ran upward from the side of the house, sirens screaming as they chased the Cherokee.

The three in the entry room looked at one another. Elkins said, "I'd say, we lost our ride."

10

Downhill," Parker said. "And time to switch."

The orange coats were reversible, muddy brown waterproofs on the other side. As they trotted through the house, headed now for the front entrance, they shook off the coats, pulled the sleeves through, shrugged into the coats again, switched their guns from the inner pockets to the out.

Bert Hayes, crawling on his stomach, had made it halfway through the doorway, heading back into the office, probably hoping to knock the phone off the desk. Moxon, lying where they'd left him, looked up, startled, as they jumped over Hayes's legs and stopped for one second at the front door. Parker pulled the door open just far enough to see out, to be sure there were no vehicles and no people out there, only the two-lane concrete road angling away downhill.

"Good," he said, and they went out, and straight down the hill.

Panting as he ran, trying to talk, Wiss said, "There'll be more coming up. They'll call for backup."

"We go as far as we can," Parker said, "then get off the road, work downhill."

"Lights!" Elkins called, and all three veered away from the road, running full tilt in among the evergreens, as the flashing red lights came thrusting up the hill. They dropped to the ground, saw and heard the three state police cars go by, and waited until the sirens were only echoes from up the mountain. Then they got to their feet, and Parker said, "We can do the road again for a while. They're all up there, they've got Harry to think about, they won't start back down—"

"Until Moxon and Hayes start talking," Elkins said.

"We've got a few minutes, anyway," Parker told him, "and the road's faster."

They loped downhill for less than a minute when Elkins yelled, "Another one!" and again they hurried away from the road. But this time Parker went only as far as the cover of the first tree, because there was something wrong with it, whatever that was coming up the road.

A big vehicle, boxy, almost completely white. But no whirling red lights, not even headlights, and no siren. Just—

Wiss, peering from nearby, said, "An ambulance? So soon?"

"Hold on," Parker said, and got to his feet, and trotted toward the road as the ambulance went by, moving slow, without extra light or sound. "Lloyd!" he yelled, and the driver turned his white face, saw Parker waving his arms, and the brake lights flashed on.

"My God," Wiss yelled, "it's Larry!"

They ran toward the ambulance, as Lloyd rolled down his window to shout, "One in front, two in back!" He was dressed in a white coat but no hat, like a medic.

Wiss climbed in front with Lloyd, the other two in back, where there was a narrow long space between two made-up stretchers. Parker sat on the right, Elkins on the left.

Wiss slammed his door and then, astonished, said, "Larry? What the hell are you *doing?*"

"I figured," Lloyd said, "I'd see how you guys were, if everything was okay we could carry the paintings in the back." Looking in his interior mirror, he said, "You two set back there?"

"Turn it around," Parker told him. "Get us out of here."

Lloyd's jaw dropped. "What? We need those paintings!"

Wiss said, "Larry, there's law all over that place up there."

"No," Lloyd said. The muscles of his jaw were bunched. "That's the only score I've got. I need to do my face, I need to set myself up."

"Larry," Elkins said, "let's discuss this a hundred miles from here."

"I can't leave this mountain without the paintings," Lloyd insisted. He sat hunched over the steering wheel, glaring sidelong at Wiss.

Mildly, Parker said to Wiss, "Ralph, he's beginning to sound like those other friends of yours."

"Wait, wait a minute," Wiss said. "Let's talk this over."

"Not here," Parker said.

"I tell you what," Wiss said. "The sentry house, just down the road. There's nobody in there now, no reason for anybody to go there. We can move ourselves in just long enough to talk."

Parker said, "Just so we're moving away from the lodge."

"Exactly." Wiss said to Lloyd, "Do it, Larry."

Lloyd unclenched. "Fine," he said.

As Lloyd K-turned the blocky ambulance, Elkins said, "Going down, Larry, use your flasher and siren. There's gonna be more cops coming up."

"I'm not sure where those controls are," Lloyd said.

Wiss told him, "You drive, I'll find them," and leaned close to the dashboard.

As they started down the slope, Elkins said, "How do you manage to promote yourself an ambulance?"

"The hospital was only a few blocks from the motel," Lloyd explained, "and this was parked by itself."

Ahead, two more state cars were coming up. Wiss

ducked low, and the state cars pulled to the side to let the ambulance roar on by.

A minute later they saw the sentry house down below them, to the left of the road, with the driveway angling in toward the wide three-car attached garage. As Wiss cut the siren and lights and Lloyd slowed for the turn, Parker said, "Cut over the lawn, take it around back, where they won't see it from the road."

Lloyd said, "What about the garage?"

"Later, if we have to. Now, we'd have to bust in, and we can't bust into this building."

As Lloyd steered the ambulance around the sentry house, Wiss said, "That's right, this place is still wired, we could set off alarms down in the police station in Havre."

"We'll ease in," Elkins said. "The house won't even know we're there."

Lloyd stopped the ambulance close to the rear of the house. He reached for his door, but stopped when Parker said, "Lloyd."

Lloyd looked around at him. He looked apprehensive, but determined. "Yes?"

Parker said, "I don't like to leave empty-handed either, but it would be worse to leave in a prison bus. If we work something out, good. If not, I don't mind leaving you right here."

Lloyd slowly nodded. "I understand," he said.

11

Wiss did the easing, through the back door. He took nearly ten minutes at it, and during that time more cars ran up the road, invisible from here, and two ran down it. Then finally Wiss said, "*There* you are, you son of a bitch," and the door swung open.

Not yet noon on a bright but sunless day; they didn't need a light to find their way around the rooms. This was a much more utilitarian structure, with a simple kitchen and dining room, a combination living room and recreation room with sofas and a Ping-Pong table and television set and bookshelves, plus the security room, all downstairs. They didn't bother to go upstairs, which was presumably all bedrooms, but clustered into the security room.

The alarm systems were all still functioning. Eighteen monitors showed the inside and outside of the lodge, and another cluster of twelve monitors showed the views from the perimeter cameras. They stood and looked at the different pictures of the lodge, and every one of them was crawling with police.

"Bad guys go in," Elkins commented, "but bad guys don't come out."

"There's no cameras in the basement," Wiss said. "We don't know if they got in the gallery or not."

A small black delivery van appeared on the down-hill perimeter monitors, then the exterior house monitors as it drove on by, then the uphill monitors. "So Harry didn't make it," Elkins said.

Lloyd was confused. "Why? What was that?"

"Morgue car," Wiss told him, and a black body bag appeared on the house monitors, carried to the front door by four state troopers. "And that," Wiss said, "is Bob, to go with him."

Parker turned away from the screens. "Time to talk this out."

They moved to the living room, sat on the sofas and chairs, and Lloyd said, "The great advantage is, we can watch what they're doing, and they have no idea we're here."

Parker said, "There's at least thirty cops in that place, with more coming. A painting in a crate is too big and heavy to sneak out. It doesn't matter if you can watch them, and we don't know when somebody's gonna decide to make this place their headquarters."

Elkins said, "That won't happen, Parker, the action's up there."

"I'll watch the monitors," Lloyd offered. "If it looks

like they're coming down here, I'll warn you, and I'll let you know if anything useful happens."

Parker looked over at the window. "It gets dark here around five," he said. "That's when we leave."

Lloyd was unhappy with that, but all he said was, "We'll work it out before then, I know we will." Rising, he said, "I'll go watch," and left the room.

The other three were silent for a couple of minutes, and then Wiss said, "I know Larry's pressing a little hard, Parker, but he's not like Bob and Harry."

"Fine," Parker said.

"When the time comes," Wiss said, "he'll be okay, I'll vouch for him."

Parker looked at Wiss. "Don't vouch for him," he said.

"Wrong word, Ralph," Elkins said.

Wiss looked uncomfortable. "I'm just saying he'll be okay."

"But don't tie yourself to him," Parker said. "If he's gonna be unhappy, I'm not gonna leave him behind me."

"I understand," Wiss said. "If it comes to that, believe me, he's on his own."

12

A little after three o'clock, Lloyd came into the living room. He was wearing a brown uniform from one of the security people here, and he carried a liquor carton half-filled with a jumble of electronic gear, like a failed high school science project. He put the box on the Ping-Pong table and said, "I've got it figured out."

They watched him. Nobody said anything.

Lloyd said, "I looked, and there's one Blazer left in the garage here. About an hour ago, they brought the paintings up, in the crates, stacked them in the front hall. Obviously, they're waiting for transportation."

Wiss said, "Larry, they're not gonna believe the Blazer is their transportation."

"That's not my idea," Lloyd said. He was very earnest, as though he were describing a new Internet application. "When we see their truck go up, when we see them start loading, I follow, in the Blazer, I say, 'Hi,

I'm Dave Rappleyea, need any help here?' We don't need every last painting, you know. Whatever's in it when I get there, I grab the truck and drive down."

Wiss said, "Larry, you'll never get away with that."

"Listen to me," Lloyd insisted. "You'll be able to watch me on the screens, and the minute I take off in the truck, you shut off their electricity and their phone, I can show you how."

Elkins said, "Larry, they can still radio."

Lloyd pointed to the junk in the cardboard carton. "I made a jammer," he said. "You douse their phone and electric, come in here, you see the two dangling wires? You twist them together, no radios on this mountain."

Parker said, "Police cars go faster than trucks."

"I can get this far," Lloyd told him. "We'll have the ambulance beside the road, just up at the next curve, there's oxygen canisters in there, we can turn the ambulance into a bomb. You put the ambulance in the middle of the road right after I go by, get into the truck with me, the ambulance blows, they can't follow us or see us or radio anybody or do anything, and we're long gone."

"Larry," Wiss said, "none of that is gonna work. They'll have you in cuffs the minute you're out of the Blazer."

"Why would they? They know what the security people here look like, and what the Blazer is."

Elkins said, "Larry, I never knew you had yourself confused with James Bond."

Lloyd offered a shaky grin. "Are you kidding? The last few weeks, I've been scaling cliffs, shooting people, getting rid of bodies, stealing ambulances, I *am* James Bond." Earnest again, he turned back to Wiss. "Ralph, it's my only shot at those paintings, and without those paintings I'm dead, even if Mr. Parker here *doesn't* kill me."

Wiss blinked. He and Elkins looked at Parker, who looked at Lloyd, whose expression was now that of a kid in the principal's office, insisting they got the wrong guy.

Parker said, "Take your shot."

13

Parker, watching the Blazer appear on the downhill monitors, said, "I'm sorry I had to leave the Remington."

Wiss was out positioning the ambulance, while Elkins and Parker watched the monitors. Elkins looked away from the screens to study Parker's profile. "Why?"

Parker nodded at the Blazer just as it ran beyond the range of the downhill monitors. "If they grab him, and they might, what does he say about you and me? He has a history, he talks with prosecutors. If I had the Remington, I'd drop him when they drive him down past here. Whatever Ralph thinks."

The Blazer appeared on the exterior house monitors, coming up. Uniformed cops, four of them, carried one crate at a time out of the lodge and up the ramp and into the back of the tall slat-sided canvas-covered truck with the state police logo on both doors. The driver, smoking a cigarette, wandered around the front of the building, curious, looking the place over. Inside, in various rooms, uniformed and plainclothes cops conducted a detailed search, a fishing expedition they could play at because the place was already a crime scene.

Elkins said, "Ralph won't argue. We all know Larry; he's okay, but he gets too emotional."

Moxon had established himself in the office near the front door. Parker watched him look out the window, see the Blazer coming, and get to his feet. He walked out of the lodge as the four cops were coming in for another crate.

Moxon stepped down off the porch, and Lloyd got smiling out of the Blazer, walking forward to meet Moxon, hand held out, mouth already moving. Moxon seemed a little confused, but not suspicious, and accepted the handshake.

Elkins said, "He's making it work."

Moxon and Lloyd stood together, near the left side of the truck, talking, Lloyd making gestures down the hill, explaining himself.

"The reason he can do a civilian so good," Elkins said, "is because he *is* a civilian."

On the screens, Moxon made a right-arm gesture that clearly invited Lloyd into the lodge, come on in, sit in the office, let's figure out who you are and what you're doing here. Lloyd, smiling, eager, did his own gesture: you first. Moxon turned toward the house, and Lloyd jumped into the truck as the four cops were coming out again, toting another crate.

"God *damn!*" Elkins said.

Moxon turned, yelling, jumping toward the truck, but Lloyd already had it rolling. It faced downhill, so all he had to do was put it in neutral to get it to move.

They watched Moxon run beside the truck, shouting, almost reaching the door handle, but then the truck jerked forward as Lloyd got the engine started, and a second later it leaped away, leaving Moxon behind.

"Son of a bitch did it," Elkins said.

Moxon turned to yell toward the house. The four cops had dropped the crate and were running for the nearby parked police cars. The truck ran away downhill from the house and its monitors, disappearing as the cops, in two police cars, raced after it.

Parker hit the switches Lloyd had marked to cut the lodge's power and phone. "Jam it," he said, and Elkins hurried out of the room toward the jammer Lloyd had made.

Parker watched the truck, not fast, appear in the downhill monitors. Already the two police cars were closing with it. He left the security room, found Elkins coming in the hall outside, and said, "Come on. It's going bad."

They trotted from the house, Elkins saying, "What's up?"

"The truck's too slow, there won't be a gap where we could block the road."

Wiss was in the ambulance, motor running. They had it sideways on the road, blocking the uphill lane, its rear in the middle of the road. The passenger side faced downhill, two tall green oxygen canisters angled out the open passenger window.

Parker shouted to Wiss, "Come out! Leave the engine on!"

Wiss clambered out of the ambulance and met Parker and Elkins in front of it, saying, "What's wrong?"

"Truck too slow," Parker told him, "cops right on his tail. You two get down to the next curve, flag Lloyd down, I'll get there."

He went around to get into the ambulance, as the other two trotted away. He was positioned at the downhill end of a tight curve, flanked by thick evergreens. The truck would be almost on him before anybody saw anybody.

He heard sirens, getting louder. Why did they bother with sirens? But it told him they were close. He shifted into reverse.

The truck swerved around the curve, rocking from side to side, motor loudly straining, going as fast as it could, which wasn't fast enough. Lloyd, a pale shape behind the windshield, bounced like a puppet inside there, twisting the wheel back and forth. The police cars, in a row, streamed right behind him.

The truck roared by the ambulance and Parker stamped hard on the accelerator. The ambulance surged backward, ramming the first police car just behind its left front wheel, bouncing it off the road. The second police car, swerving away from the ambulance that now blocked the entire road, ran into a tree on the other side.

Parker shifted into drive, and the ambulance jounced forward, accelerating around the next curve, finding the truck stopped there, just off the road. He pounded the brake pedal, skewed to a sideways stop, reaching to spin both oxygen canister valves open, then jumped out of the ambulance and ran for the truck.

They were already firing at the oxygen when he got there. It took half a dozen shots before a ricochet caused the spark they needed. Then the explosion pinned them against the side of the truck, threw heat at them and then wind, and then cold.

The ambulance was a mass of debris now, spread across the road. Trees to both sides had caught fire.

14

The state road was just ahead, their motel a dozen miles to the right. "Turn left," Parker said.

Lloyd, at the wheel, didn't argue. The four of them were crammed shoulder to shoulder on the bench seat of the truck, Parker next to the right door, ducking his head from time to time to look in the outside mirror. But there was no pursuit, and nothing to block them at the intersection up ahead. The cops up at the lodge couldn't get out, and they couldn't ask for help. Parker and the others had an hour, maybe more.

Lloyd took the left, a little too fast, and Wiss, next to him, said, "Take it easy, Larry. Nobody's chasing us now."

"Okay. Okay."

Parker said, "If we go slow, nobody looks at us. Ralph, if we drop you at the next town, can you get yourself a car?"

"Sure," Wiss said. "You want me to go back to the motel? Will do. I get Frank's car and our stuff, and where'll you people be?"

"After the town," Parker said, "we'll take the first dead end on the left. We'll be up in there some place."

"There's a town coming up," Lloyd said. He was trying to be calm, but his voice jittered as though he were being shaken, and his fingers kept flexing on the wheel.

It was a small one-traffic-light town. The light turned green in front of them, so Lloyd rolled through the intersection and pulled to the curb on the far side. He said, "Maybe somebody else can drive."

"I will," Elkins said.

"Good."

Lloyd opened his door and climbed down out of the truck, followed by Wiss, who shut the door. Lloyd, still in his brown security uniform, trotted around the front of the truck as Elkins and Parker both moved along the seat to their left. Wiss strolled away, hands in his pockets, and Lloyd got up onto the seat next to Parker. His grin flickered, like a lightbulb about to blow. Shutting his door, he said, "I'm beginning to feel the aftereffects." His teeth were chattering.

"That's okay," Parker told him, as Elkins put the truck in gear. "Shake it out."

Lloyd did. Next to Parker, he twitched as though electric currents were running through him. "I was okay while it was going on," he said, "but now?" He held his shaking hand up and looked at it. "I don't think I could write my name."

"You don't have to," Elkins told him, "so don't worry about it."

The first road on the left with a sign reading DEAD END was a narrow two lanes, dirt. A low wooden prefab house at the corner had swings and toys all around it, but a quarter mile up the road the evergreens started. When they got up that far, in among the trees, Parker said, "Stop here."

Deep drainage ditches ran on both sides of the road, dry now, for the spring thaws. Elkins stopped pretty much in the middle of the road, and all three got out to walk around back to see what they had.

Four crates. "Not many," Lloyd said.

Elkins said, "Larry, that fella Marino had a very good eye. It doesn't matter which four these are, they'll buy you a dozen new faces."

"One will do me."

No two crates were the same size, but all were very heavy. They wrestled them out of the truck one at a time, then slid them down into the right-hand drainage ditch, hauled them up the other side, and shoved them flat as far as possible under low ever-green branches. Then Parker said to Elkins, "Drive it on up a couple miles, somewhere you can get it off the road. We'll wait here."

"Fine."

Elkins turned, about to jump across the ditch, but

then paused to look back at Parker and said, "Larry did good."

"He did fine," Parker agreed.

Elkins met his eyes for a minute, then shrugged and said, "That's okay, then," and jumped the ditch.

As Elkins drove the truck farther up the road, Parker sat on a protruding corner of crate. "Now we wait," he said.

"I'm not even cold," Lloyd said.

"Uh-huh."

Parker sat looking at the road, listening to the faint rustle of the woods. It would be an hour, maybe more, before Wiss got here. They could drop Parker at the airport in Bismarck, North Dakota, on their way home to Chicago, he'd take a plane east, call Claire.

Lloyd said, "I'm too jumpy to sit." He walked back and forth, back and forth, looking at the road, looking with wonder at his own hands. Finally, he stopped to face Parker and say, "So you aren't going to do it."

"No need," Parker said.

"Good." Lloyd gazed around at the woods, calmer now, smiling at the day. "Smell the trees," he said. "That's a great smell."